Born in Cork in 1954, Dr Richard Kearney is a Professor of Philosophy at University College, Dublin. He has written and edited twenty books on philosophy and literature including, most recently, STATES OF MIND and POETICS OF MODERNITY. He has also presented *Visions of Europe*, *L'autre Irlande*, and *The Book Programme* for Irish and European television. SAM'S FALL is his first novel. He is married with two children.

SCEPTRE

Sam's
Fall

RICHARD KEARNEY

SCEPTRE

First published in 1995 by Hodder and Stoughton
A division of Hodder Headline PLC
A Sceptre Paperback

10 9 8 7 6 5 4 3 2 1

British Library Cataloguing in Publication Data

Kearney, Richard
  Sam's Fall
  I. Title
  823 [F]

ISBN 0 340 66082 1

Typeset by Palimpsest Book Production Limited,
Polmont, Stirlingshire
Printed and bound in Great Britain by
Cox and Wyman Ltd, Reading, Berkshire

Hodder and Stoughton
A division of Hodder Headline PLC
338 Euston Road
London NW1 3BH

For Anne

∫

'If on my account this storm is upon you, take me and cast me into the sea, that this tempest may recede; yet let it first be your part like those mariners to seek to save the shipwrecked by the bowels of godliness, and to draw the ship to land, as they did according to the scripture, which says, And the men sought to return to land and could not, for the sea ran and the swell increased the more.'

The Works of St Columbanus, Epistula II, AD 603

Head to head. As it must have been just before the beginning. Two as one. Then both at once struggling for space, to be free of the other, and the rush of air and that terrible light outside, as they burst apart. Brothers.

Head to head, again, now. But this time Sam is dead. Space again, but this time it's all Jack's – his brother is gone, back to the dark. Only a sliver of coffin separates them, as Jack carries his brother shoulder-high down the length of the aisle. As near now as they ever were in life.

Jack imagines Sam whispering through the panel of gleaming wood. There is whispering, but of course it is not Sam. It is the monks, no doubt. Sam's other brothers. Not real ones; Jack is the only real one. But *brothers in Christ*. Three Cistercian novices, the other bearers of Sam's coffin, moving with Jack in slow, sandalled steps towards the altar. They didn't call him Sam. These brothers called him by his novice name – Tobias. *Brother Tobias*. Jack will stick to the first name, his brother's real name – Sam, *Samuel Toland*.

Nearing the altar, Jack notices Raphaëlle crying. Her head is bent, her grieving deep and muffled. He can tell by her ragged breathing. Mouth half open, eyes half closed. But why should Jack's fiancée grieve so for Sam, who had always seemed so cold towards her? Even when he came to spend those summer breaks in Myrtleville, or travelled with them to Paris and St Gallen. Jack had tried to smooth things, but Sam was so obsessed with his research he scarcely listened when Raphaëlle spoke. He showed no interest in her photography. They didn't speak the same language. Sam had ears only for the word of God. He'd say so himself, half joking. For God and Abbot Anselm.

Anselm. That towering monk with pale eyes and huge hands, whom Jack and Sam had both revered since boyhood, from the moment they first arrived as boarding students in this Abbey. The way he stood out from the curtained platform at Assembly and introduced himself, all those years ago, awesome in voice and stature, mind bent on some ineffable thing, his words of promise lifting the boys across the threshold into a new home, provoking a strange ache of recognition. And there he stands again now, before another assembly, Abbot Anselm welcoming Sam once more, for one final blessing.

Anselm awaits the coffin as the bearers pass through the gilded gates on to the strip of washed-blue carpet leading to the altar. Minister of rites, doctor of souls, director of Columbanus Abbey – Sam's second home, the home he never left. Today, magnificent in purple alb, white stole, Anselm radiates light within the circle of black-robed monks. A space lit from within like a scooped oyster shell. Anselm opens his arms and spreads his hands as the coffin is set on the stand before him. The Abbot's eyes close. The reading is from Psalm 139.

Whither shall I go from thy spirit, whither shall I flee from thy presence? If I take the wings of the morning and dwell in the uttermost parts of the sea, even there shall thy hand lead me, and thy hand shall hold me.

They think they own Sam now, these cowled, whey-faced men. But they are wrong. *Brother Tobias* is theirs, not *Samuel Toland*. They know nothing of him, of the real Sam, Jack's brother. He is Jack's again now.

The Abbey choir keeps vigil from the wooden stalls, intoning verses of the liturgy of St John Chrysostom. When it ends Anselm steps towards Sam's coffin and traces a small cross in the air with his right hand. '*Dominus vobiscum*,' he chants equably, looking at nothing. 'Blessed is the soul wounded by love, for in its wounding it is always healed,' he sings again, the prayer of Columbanus, his face still revealing nothing.

Raphaëlle is lying in bed in the Abbey guest room, her eyes turned away from Jack towards the white wall. Jack says, 'I think I'll stay on here for a while.'

Raphaëlle's face muscles tighten, but she says nothing.

Jack stands tall and square-shouldered on the brown linoleum, making no sounds; he reaches out for a leather bag at the end of the bed and removes a pair of pyjamas.

Raphaëlle curls closer into herself, pulling the beige blanket over a bare shoulder.

Jack knows those blankets, the harshness of the cloth against the skin. Every night for years he'd wrapped them about him in beds like this. Junior Dorm, Inter Dorm, Senior Dorm. All those years he'd spent here in the Abbey with Sam, before he left, leaving Sam behind to pursue his vocation.

Breathing in the familiar air of the room, he is surprised to find his heart raging, the initial numbing occasioned by the news of Sam's death and the subsequent succession of funeral arrangements yielding to a feeling of terrible loss. His steps are fretful as he begins to pace the floor. He lets his mind coast.

Why had Sam died like that? When he seemed so set in his calling, so sure of his novitiate? Unlike Jack, he had sustained the Abbot's guidance, suspended all attachments to the splendours of the world, followed his vocation through. Unlike Jack, whose precipitous expulsion from the Abbey came after a moment of stolen bliss in the forest! *Her beauty like the olive tree, her fragrance like that of Lebanon, flourishing as a garden, as the forests and vineyards of Lebanon.* Over three years ago that was. His misdemeanour, yes, his parting of ways with Sam.

How different their lives had grown since. Only one week ago Sam was making last preparations for Final Vows while Jack got news of his BA degree in Botany and made plans with Raphaëlle for the wedding in Geneva. Raphaëlle. The ultimate and ineluctable difference between Jack and Sam. Raphaëlle, lying there now, her face inclined towards the wall, immobile. Jack moves towards her, resting his arms loosely on her shoulders.

Raphaëlle turns towards Jack. 'You never did believe in Sam's vocation, did you?' She speaks evenly.

Jack draws back, looks away. His shoulders hunch a little.

'I'm not sure.' He pauses. 'It could have been me, you know. Anselm thought at first that I would be the one . . .'

'You never told me.' Raphaëlle catches his eye with unnerving directness.

'It never came up. All that was over by the time I met you. Anselm had his hopes for me when I was in school. He'd prepared me, in a way, before Sam. But fate put paid to that . . .'

'When you were expelled?'

'Yes. Anselm was shaken, but could do nothing . . . Then Sam discovered his vocation –' Jack breaks off.

'I don't want you to stay on here, Jack. You know

we're expected in Geneva.' Raphaëlle's tone betrays her alarm.

He doesn't meet her eyes. 'Just a few days,' he says lightly. 'I need to help Anselm with Sam's papers . . .'

'He doesn't need you for that. He knows Sam's work on the *Priscian* better than anyone.' Raphaëlle crinkles her green eyes, her voice vaguely belligerent.

'It's not just the *Priscian*, Raphaëlle. Sam was working on something else.'

'What?' Raphaëlle's tone softens. She steadies her gaze until Jack meets it.

'A kind of journal. I noticed it yesterday when Anselm and I were going through some things Sam left behind in Myrtleville. Anselm told me it was part of Sam's 'personal itinerary'. It's called *The Life of Tobias*. There's an odd cut-out picture of a horse on the cover, and a dedication to Anselm.'

'What's in it?'

'I didn't have time to find out. Anselm suggested I stay on here a while to read it.' Jack looks towards the window. 'He said it might help me understand things better . . .'

Raphaëlle stares, then turns away again.

Jack watches her body shift beneath the blanket. A deep sound rises up from inside her, muffled and half blocked at first, then audible, almost a moan.

'What is it?' Jack asks.

Raphaëlle doesn't answer.

'What's wrong with you?' he asks again, bewildered by this unbidden show of grief and irritated at the tone of his own voice.

Still she says nothing. Her shoulders shudder slightly beneath the bedclothes.

Jack tries to gather himself, his glance lighting upon the eyes of the icon mounted on the opposite wall. The Angel of St Gallen, a replica of the original from the Icon Chamber beneath the church, leitmotif of Columbanus Abbey, gazes back at him. White wrinkles of cracked paint run like tiny tributaries over the dark-ringed eyes, single-stroke nose, small mouth and tan-flecked cheeks. Accusing eyes? Inviting eyes? Is that a frown passing over the face? A half-smile?

Jack turns back to Raphaëlle. 'I know why Sam entered the Abbey,' he says after a pause. 'It was because of Anselm. I don't think you can understand what he meant to us. Sam gave up everything for him.'

Raphaëlle raises herself to lean on one elbow. 'Everything?' she challenges.

Jack flinches. But he doesn't relent. 'Yes. Everything.' He blinks for a moment, his eyes dilating, as he brushes his thick red hair back from his forehead. 'It's not something I can explain right now. I need to stay here for a while and think things through.'

'Don't, Jack. Please.' Raphaëlle struggles unsuccessfully for composure. 'I want you with me,' she says, the space around her suddenly inhospitable. 'I don't trust Anselm.'

'You don't know Anselm.' Jack replies vehemently. 'You don't know how he cared for us, taught us things, sacred things, special ways to know ourselves, to listen to the voice . . .'

'Whose voice?'

Jack lets Raphaëlle's question hang unanswered.

'I need some air,' he says. 'I'll see you later.'

Raphaëlle stares uneasily at Jack's retreating figure, the shade veiling his face as he steps back and closes the door behind him.

III

It is cooler out in the flagstoned corridor. Jack sees nothing at first, but he knows this walk by heart. His feet move all on their own, the echo of his steps familiar, as he passes through the archway from the school wing into the Abbey's cloisters. How often he had followed this same path as a boarder, to seek out Anselm in his room, looking for counsel, confiding things, confessing doubts.

A flash of moonlight skims across a window, outlining the profile of tall oaks. The soft dark returns then, beckoning Jack into the monks' granite-grey quarters. If the Abbot's light is on, Jack will knock. But Anselm's light is not on. Jack calls his name, but there is no reply. He hesitates. A narrow bar of light gleams farther down the corridor. He walks towards it, as though following a sign, to a door of dark-grained oak. The name, *Brother Tobias*, is inscribed in copperplate. Jack knocks. There is no answer. He pushes the iron handle and the door opens wide. There is no one inside, though a desk-lamp lights the room. He shouldn't go in, he knows. Sam's second home. Celibate cell for three years of his life.

The room is empty but for a few spare things, bed,

work-table, chair, icon, shelf. A neat selection of books lines the front of Sam's desk, illuminated by the small lamp, set out, as if arranged for someone. The space is cramped, neat and austere. The walls are whitewashed, like all the walls in the Abbey. Jack sits on the narrow bed, with the same iron frame and beige blanket as the guest room and dormitories. He imagines he has been here before, though he has not. He imagines raucous voices of schoolboys rising up from the dark yard outside. He imagines huge clouds piling up on the horizon of oak woods flanking the Abbey, climbing like coils of silver into the glassy air – though he sees nothing.

After a while, Jack begins to see what *is* there. On one wall, a black and white woodcut of the old town of St Gallen with the words *Verbum Domini Manet Internum* inscribed above it. On the other, a small-scale print of the Angel of St Gallen gazing down at him from above Sam's shelf. Jack moves from the bed to Sam's desk. The chair is sturdy. He glances through the titles on the shelf in front of him. Old and New Testaments. Church Fathers. Augustine's *Confessions. Summa Theologica. The Works of St Columbanus*. Eckhart's *Sermons*. Then a cluster of paperbacks – *David Copperfield. Narziss and Goldmund. Mephisto. Joseph and His Brothers*. And, finally, at the far end, the row of files entitled 'Notes towards a Revised Edition of the Priscian Grammar' by Brother Tobias Toland. The research thesis Sam had been working on for three years, ever since he entered the novitiate. 'The Edition' Sam was for ever on about in that measured *sotto voce* tone of his. He always brought some piece of the research with him on holidays. Obscure articles on tenth-century calligraphy and early Irish scripts. He'd spend hours writing and rewriting commentaries. Up to the very end, he never stopped going on about it – the quest for the perfect language, the ideal grammar, the alphabet of the Tongue of Tongues which existed before Babel, before the Fall, before Creation itself. He was completely obsessed.

Then Jack notices Sam's other book, the journal, a dappled, leather-bound copybook tucked away beside the research files. Anselm must have put it back there, in its place on Sam's shelf, where it belonged. Jack takes it in both hands and lays it square on the desk in front of him. The title – *The Life of Tobias* – is meticulously inscribed in Sam's inimitable copperplate. An extract from the *Rule of Columbanus* follows the dedication to Anselm: *For Anselm: 'Ask Thy Father and he will show you. A person without a confessor is like a person without a head!'* The picture of the horse, carefully pasted on to the cover, stares out at Jack. A wrinkled drawing, coloured in with bold sweeping strokes, as though in a child's hand. Jack opens the first page.

THE LIFE OF TOBIAS

PART ONE

'For a child is humble, does not harbour the remembrance of injury, does not lust after a woman when he looks on her, does not keep one thing on his lips and another in his heart. And these, as I have said, will be better maintained by one who is still and sees that God Himself is Lord, than by one who sees and hears all manner of things.'

The Works of St Columbanus, Epistula II, 8. AD 603

∫

The sand was hot. My feet burned, like my peeling
shoulders. I smelled of the white suncream Mother had just
rubbed on to me, her hand cold and wet from the sea.

I ran towards the shiny water.

Water. Water.

'No, Sam!' I heard her cry out behind me. 'Sam, come
back!'

Freezing streams of grainy sand rushed between my toes,
slipping beneath me, sucking away from me, back into the
sea, a gleaming wet carpet, inviting me in.

'Come back, Sam!'

Water.

It was curling towards me now. The wave. A huge belly
of water, hollow in the middle. Bluey-black flowing skin
breaking into arms of foam. Then it was all over me –
turning and tussling out of control – all white, all noise,
like the noise inside a seashell, like the noise on a radio
between stations, crackling a distant roar.

My mouth, wide open, filled with sea.

I couldn't cry. I couldn't speak.

Water.

Entry 2
Cork, November 1959

Her smell filled the bedroom, it was gorgeous. As she bent down to kiss me, her perfume hanging in the air, a halo around me. All mine, for a second, as she bent down to kiss me.

The smell of her dress was a mix of all those tiny coloured bottles on her dressing table. I didn't know the names. But I knew her hair and neck smelled like her favourite perfume. She'd just come up for a moment, she said, to tuck her 'little ones' into bed. I was one of her little ones. Jack was the other.

She left again, but her smell stayed. Breathing in, I could keep her with me just a little longer, as the bedroom door closed behind her, and the light from the landing narrowed and was gone. Angela, she was called. Angela Toland. She was my mother.

She was Jack's mother too. Jack, my brother. We were born on the same day, but I had a hole in the heart and spent much of my first year in hospital. So Jack was always that bit ahead. People called us the Toland Twins, and said we were inseparable, which was part of the problem. There were two of us to one of her. And I wanted her all to myself.

Jack was not his real name. His real name was John. John Toland. But we called him Jack – for short, although Jack was no shorter than John. I was never sure, in fact, why we called him Jack, but I think it had something to do with the fact that his favourite rhymes were all about boys called Jack – *Jeepers Jack my shirt is black – Jack and Jill went up the hill – Frère Jacques*, or our father's story of *Jacky Dory*.

Our Father, just like the prayer said, except he wasn't

in heaven. He was on earth. He wasn't home much. He was off doing operations in The Eye and Ear most of the time. Or else he was in his rooms in Sydney Parade with people queuing to see him. Our father was an Eye Doctor. But I liked to think of him as a knight on some perilous Crusade, miles from home, smelling of wounds and nuns and antiseptic. I liked him best like that, the King far away, King Richard the Lion Heart. Mother, Maid Marion. Jack, the Sheriff of Nottingham. Me, Robin.

Sometimes Mother had me and Jack kneel by our beds at prayer-time and ask God to guide Father's needle as he tried to save the sight of hopeless cases – the little boy from Mayfield who lost his eye in a catapult fight, the lady from Douglas who fell down the stairs and burst an eyeball, the messenger man from Madden's who went blind when his bike hit a bus, the garda on point duty at the South Mall run over by the Protestant Lady doctor. Yes, I loved our father when we prayed for all the suffering ones who kept him out at night, operating. I could see their split veins, bleeding tubes, broken face bones – just like in the big leather medical books we weren't allowed to look at. Particularly the ones with pictures of the cloudy eye disease that makes you blind – *glaucoma*. I prayed that Father would cure each of his patients, one after the other, and that it would take ages. Hours and hours. I loved him most when he wasn't there.

Jack was there all of the time. And the worst thing was he learned to do joined writing before I did. One afternoon, he spent hours crossing letters to make up words, rows upon rows of them. He moved his tongue around his lips when he did each line, his hand moving across the page and back, really slow. He just kept on doing it, sitting at the desk in the drawing room, making messages on Father's special notepaper, the one with blue letters on top. '*Dr Joseph Toland. Sydney Parade, Cork, Telephone: 66221.*'

Jack wasn't writing to Father today, though. He said it was secret. But I knew.

Jack could make letters and I couldn't. He could make words appear on paper just by drawing lines and crossing them in special ways. But these letters could carry messages even when he wasn't there. Jack told me he could put them in an envelope and leave them for someone to read, and that that *someone* would know what the letters said. Jack didn't have to be there for his words to speak. They could speak to someone, even if Jack was dead.

Jack didn't say who that *someone* was, but I knew. And I couldn't stop thinking of Jack putting that secret message under her pillow, then going away, and her coming into her bedroom and finding it there, and reading it, all alone; and then he'd have her all to himself.

I'd have to think of something else. As soon as Jack was asleep that night, I crept from my bed to his side of the room, took the colouring book and pencils from under his bed and sneaked out on to the landing. I sat on the red carpet and opened Jack's book at the page with the black and white horse. It wouldn't take long.

I pulled the picture from the book, careful not to tear it, put a clean piece of paper over it and traced the head of the horse, detail by detail, until it came through, like the magic face on a pound note held up against the light, or like one of the pictures Mother painted by her bedroom window in summer. *Aquarelles*, she called them. *Aquarelles*. I didn't know what it meant, but it sounded like something in a prayer, full of colours, with no words.

I coloured in the horse with pencils, the hidden thing coming towards me through the paper, as if it was *really* there. The Irish horse that won the Cheltenham Cup. Roddy Owen!

I was ready now. The red stairs down to the drawing room had never been this red. I walked to the white door, the picture held in one hand as I turned the knob. The noise inside was very loud.

I couldn't see anyone at first, with all the legs. But Uncle Dick saw me. I'd bumped straight into his knees. He was talking to people I didn't know.

'How's little Sam, then?' he said, lifting me high with a loud laugh.

'Grand,' I said, my drawing held out in front of me.

'And did *you* do that?'

'I did. I did it myself.'

Before Uncle Dick put me down again, I saw Mother over all the heads at the other end of the room. She was standing beside the bookcase, surrounded by people.

'It's a picture of Roddy Owen,' I said out loud, to her. 'Like when he won the Gold Cup in England. It's for your birthday.'

'There's another painter in the family so,' said Aunt Madeleine as she passed the picture across to Mother. 'That's from your side of the family, Angela.'

'I won ten guineas on Roddy Owen,' Father said. He was in good humour.

'It's a beautiful picture, Sam.' My mother turned to me at last. Were her eyes laughing? Grey with green or green with grey?

'I love horses. And pictures. Especially coloured ones,' she said, approaching me. 'What a wonderful birthday present. Thank you, my love.'

There were so many things I wanted to ask her then through the parting sea of people. What does aquarelle mean? Is it as good as writing? Is it better? But my picture went dark before me.

'Look who we have here!' Father was speaking and he was not speaking to me. 'Another little artist, I suppose!' All the eyes I was looking at were now looking past me, towards the door. Someone was standing there.

Jack.

'This is impossible,' said Mother. 'This party is not for children. It's grown-up time now. You two should have been asleep long ago.'

'I was asleep,' said Jack. 'But Sam woke me up. He stole my colouring book, from under my bed.'

'I'm sure he didn't steal it,' Mother said. 'He probably just borrowed it.'

'Then why did he copy this page?' Jack held up the horse I had taken from his book.

'Sam's drawing isn't Roddy Owen,' Jack said. 'This is. Sam is just a copycat.'

'Boys!' somebody said, and others laughed and shifted their feet.

'It's still lovely,' said Mother, 'even if it is a copy. It doesn't matter. Now, both of you, say goodnight and off to bed. We don't want to see you, or hear you, again tonight. There's two good boys.'

I walked up the stairs behind Jack. The carpet was a different red, darker, like a nose bleed. I couldn't think of any words now. Except the ones from the rhyme. *Jack fell down and broke his crown.* As though someone was repeating them inside my head. *Jack fell down and broke his crown.* Just that bit, not the bits that come before and after. *Jack fell down and broke his crown.* A record stuck in the middle. I didn't remember any other words. Other words belonged to Jack.

Jack carried the book in his two hands and put it back under his bed. He got in and turned towards the wall. I got into mine. The sheets had gone cold and it was hard to warm them up again. I stared up at the black ceiling and, after a while, began to see things twisting in the dark. Rows and rows of letters curling and uncurling, lines criss-crossing over and back, stitching and unstitching, joining and unjoining to make up words. The way grown-ups did it. The way Jack did it. I would learn to do that too. I couldn't wait to learn letters now, to read letters, to write letters. No more pictures. Just letters. Joined letters with crossing lines. Yes, I would learn to spell my name. I would learn to write my name, my own name, all by myself, all for myself. *Samuel Toland. Sam* for short.

Entry 3
Cork, July 1961

We didn't see our father much, except at Sunday dinner and when he took us deep-sea fishing in the summer. He was a busy doctor, Mother always said, gone before breakfast, home after bed.

Jack and I would often hear him having supper with Mother by the drawing-room fire. We'd listen, as we lay in bed upstairs, for the noises of plates and cutlery being placed on the trolley below. We'd follow the sounds down the hall and into the drawing room, picturing the laying of the ware on the low coffee table, Father preparing the decanters and glasses on the desk by the window, then stoking the coal fire until we'd imagine it unleashing gasps of pale blue flame, and Mother placing the needle on to the spinning black edge of her favourite record. *Nocturnes.*

Jack and I knew every move by heart. Our game was to match the sounds with images. That way we played at being there with Father even though we weren't; even though we were up in bed, out of sight, prayers said, face, hands and teeth washed. We imagined Father a lot because we hardly ever saw him. Except at Sunday lunch or when he took us fishing in the summer.

Mother read bedtime stories to Jack and me before our father came home at night. *Swiss Family Robinson. Swallows*

and Amazons. The Happy Prince. We liked the last one best.
Mother took ages to finish it she always cried so much.
Jack said her tears were grey and I said green – and we
comforted her saying it was *only a story*, and she laughed
at that. It was our best time of the day, those moments
before the latch-key sounded in the hall door below and
we knew she would have to leave us.

Father never told us stories – except one, which wasn't
really a story. It was about Jacky Dory. And he stopped
telling it when Jack got mad one day. It was a Sunday. Jack
and I had followed Father from the dinner table into the
sitting room. We stood by the sloping green armchair as he
turned on the big Pye radio one of his eye patients had given
him. We'd say the names out loud as he turned the tuning
knob and the thin white switch flashed past the different
stations, each with a different voice. *Prague. Ankara. Lahti.
Paris. Nice. Lille. North. Stockh'm. Rome. West. Welsh. Berlin.
Strasbourg. Hilversum. Brussels. Athlone. Luxembourg. Light.
Hamburg. Scottish. Lisbon. Sundsvall. Geneva.* He'd always stop
at Athlone. That was where he told us Charles Mitchell
read the one o'clock news. As Father listened Jack and
I ran to the window and stared out on to the River Lee
below. We played our usual games. Spotting the tiny
figures moving about on the opposite bank by the Marina
Rowing Club, counting the number of oarsmen in each
of the long floating skiffs. Pretending we were canoeing
through Cashes and the Munster Arcade like Andy Gaw in
his punt during the big flood when the Lee burst its banks
earlier that year. Making rude rhymes about Kathy Barry
and Smelly Nelly, Dunlop's highest chimney which rose
up from the quays below and spewed smoke all day into
the Cork sky. Reciting with eyes closed the block-lettered
names of the factories lining the docks from Dunlops to
the first bridge – Fords, Gouldings, Odlums, Beamish and
Crawford, R. and H. Hall, G. W. Green and Co. Ltd, Grain

Merchants. Or aiming mock-rifles at the passengers aboard the *Innisfallen*.

Between each game we'd turn around to Father, sitting in his chair, and ask him to tell us a story.

'Once the news is over,' he'd say. But the Sunday news was never over. When the deep voice of Charles Mitchell was finished, the faraway English voice took over, more bored, more tired. Sunday news in the afternoon, like Sunday mass in the morning, went on and on. This Sunday, though, Father switched off the English announcer while he was still speaking.

We stopped our games and went over to his armchair expectantly. He folded his paper, removed his half-moon glasses and stubbed out his cigarette.

'What story would you like?' he asked us.

'The one about Jacky Dory – the man who sounds like a fish!' we said. 'But this time tell the *whole* story.'

'All right. I will tell you the story about Jacky Dory . . .' He paused, as he always paused.

'Yes, I'll tell you the story about Jacky Dory . . .' he repeated again, lighting another cigarette, lifting his glasses before he continued, '. . . and that is the end of the story.'

'That's not a *real* story! You keep leaving out the *middle* bit,' we protested.

But our father repeated it, as before. 'I'll tell you a story about Jacky Dory . . . and that is the end of the story.' Stopping between the opening line, as always, and, as always, leaving out the missing bit.

'I hate that story,' Jack cried and ran out of the room.

I followed him. I knew that if Jack couldn't get Father to finish the story, nobody could. (Jack was 'a real Toland', my mother always said: strong build and reddish hair. I was more like her, a Kiely.) We ran to Mother. She was talking to Big Nora in the kitchen. The Jacky Dory story wasn't fair, Jack sobbed. It didn't say who Jacky Dory was or where he got his name, and it never told the 'missing bit'.

Mother put her hands in the air. 'Your father's business,' she said. 'Not mine.' Jack was mad and shouted that he never wanted to be called Jack again. It was a stupid name.

But he quickly forgot his vow later that afternoon when Father called us back to the sitting room and promised to take us deep-sea fishing the following Sunday.

Entry 4
Ballycotton, August 1961

It was flat calm. We set out early enough, about ten o'clock, from Ballycotton town. We were in this big fishing trawler, thirty foot long with a high cabin, diesel engine, and gaff-rigged sail in case of emergency. Big Jim Donovan was the skipper; Packy and Joby, his two grown sons, the crew. The boat was freshly painted (there had been a great run of salmon that season). Hull coral blue, waterline red, lettering along the prow a line of brilliant white, *The Ballycotton Star*. I could just make out the words; I read the name slowly to Father. There was a sharp, sweet smell, new paint with a whiff of salmon scales.

As we motored out of the small harbour, I sat at the stern watching Jack and Father prepare the tackle; they spent ages untangling the twisted nylon lines from the previous expedition. Birds' nests, Father called them, and he stuck at it until the knots unravelled into single flowing threads. Jack was hunkered up beside him, not missing a trick, the dead spit of him with the same dark foxy hair. He'd be a deep-sea fisherman himself one day, Jack said. But I hated the smell of diesel oil and blood when they gaffed the sharks and strapped them to the gunnel. I wasn't even sure why I'd gone along that day. Maybe I thought we'd find out something about Jacky Dory?

'We'll try a drift here,' said Big Jim Donovan. He cut the engine. We were about ten miles off the Cork coast now and could barely see the town of Ballycotton against the hazy lip of shore. It was one of those terribly hot days. Jack sat beside Father as he assembled the huge rod. I came forward from the stern and sat on the other side. Father placed a bloody mackerel on a ten-inch hook and cast the bait into the sea. Meanwhile Big Jim Donovan and his two sons lowered something heavy over the stern – a massive string sack filled with sliced heads and guts of mackerel, whiting, pollock and other small fish left over from the previous day's fishing. In the water it gave off an oily slick which sharks could smell, miles away, and follow back to the bait. Rubby-dubby, they called it.

Jack spotted two fins near the slick after only a few minutes. False alarm, Big Jim said. Just dolphins on their peaceful path south. Guardian angels of shipwrecked sailors, he explained. Even been known to rescue drowning seamen; and anyone who looked into a dolphin's eye was never the same again. Something inside you changed. That's what Big Jim said.

The only other person on board was a visiting Dutch chemist, a friend of Father's who fiddled all the time with a silver pocket flask. He couldn't understand how anyone could be afraid of sharks, simple beasts of the sea! No match for man! He'd not been deep-sea fishing before. He had a little white beard along the tip of his chin. We nicknamed him The Goat.

'Have you got a bite yet, Dad?' Jack asked. He had a camera strapped over his shoulder, Mother's new Polaroid which he'd borrowed specially for the trip.

The line was well down now, slick spreading behind us like a peacock's tail. The bait lay suspended under water, its white float roller-coasting, in slow motion, on the swaying surface. Burnt engine oil and rotting rubby-dubby made an awful smell. My tummy started pushing upwards like in the swingboats with Jack at the Merries in Crosshaven, when he pulled the rope too hard. The ocean heaved more deeply with each passing swell, the sea darker and darker the further down we gazed. Jack and I were leaning right over the gunnel, following the arrows of light as they shot towards the deep, lighting up pellets of tiny plankton, blips on the radar screen beneath.

'Have you got a bite yet, Dad?' Jack asked again. The tip of the rod seemed to dip.

'Nothing,' Father replied.

'Have you caught the bottom?' Jack asked.

'Out here the ocean is bottomless,' Father said.

Big Jim Donovan nodded in agreement. The Goat laughed. We looked back towards the sea then in time to catch the reflection of two gannets, black-tipped wings outspread, curving over the water. We began to sing our sea song, the one Mother sang with us whenever we came in sight of the ocean after a long drive from the city.

> I see the sea and the sea sees me
> I see the sea and the sea sees me

For a while our voices were in such harmony you couldn't tell who was Jack and who was me. The *I* seeing the sea and the *me* being seen were one and the same.

That's when the reel screeched. The line raced through the tip of the rod now bent double, jack-knifing down into the wave. The white float bobbed furiously, went epileptic, then disappeared into the sea. Father had a bite. He yanked the rod back with all his might, all twelve stone pulling against the hidden muscle of the deep. Air escaped from his lungs as the line went taut, dead straight down beneath the boat. The shark was hooked.

Big Jim Donovan pushed aside the tangle of fishing lines he'd been unravelling. He gripped the gaff as his sons got the hand-net ready. The Goat fiddled with his pocket flask. Jack and I, we just peered down into the grey-green water, waiting for the first silver flash, for the deep-sea beast to draw towards the surface.

Father played the shark for all his worth. Or was the shark playing him? Big Jim sucked his teeth in a grin. He hadn't often seen a fight like this, he said. And he'd seen many things, especially during his days as a bell diver with the Navy during the Second War. Diving for bodies or salvage from ships sunk during fierce sea battles off Antwerp and Rotterdam where German U-boats prowled the waters. He told us all about that and the strange sharks he'd come across down there in the bilges and hulls of scuttled vessels. 'Scavengers of the deep,' he called them, 'taking their pleasure with soft-skinned corpses, ripping off chunks of limbs at one go.' The Goat was pale now, this talk of sharks too close for comfort. He laughed weakly; he didn't smile.

During a lull in the struggle, Father asked if we would like to hold the rod. I shied away, but Jack climbed on to Father's lap, slung the camera to one side, and placed his hands around the reel just above where Father kept his grip. Jack loved it, pretending to heave the shark up. But after a few seconds, the rod bucked violently again and Jack climbed back to his place beside me.

The fight went on for ages. Long enough for Big Jim to recite his diving stories and quiz Packy and Joby about what kind of shark they thought it was – porpeagle, mako, thrasher, tope, blue? I longed to know, to put a name on it, to take the fear away. With that kind of pull, said Big

Jim, it was certainly a hundred-pounder. Maybe a record for the season; the heaviest shark weighed in at Ballycotton so far that year was a ninety-pound porpeagle – when they took that one down from the scales and gutted him half a dozen dead mackerel gushed out in a slimy flood.

'I'd wager this one's bigger,' said Big Jim. His only worry was that the steel gaff wouldn't be strong enough to hold the thrashing body. But he didn't need to worry. Within yards of the gunnel, the line went dead. Not quite light or loose, just lifeless, a sort of drag. The reel turned effortlessly as father pulled in the last stretch of line. And there it was now, swinging in the air, like some hooded thing from a hangman's noose, the head of a huge porpeagle shark bitten clean off at the neck.

We could only stare. A hanging black morsel of snout, eyes, teeth and gills, blood still spurting from its gaping jugular. Big Jim was the first to break the spell. He spoke low, with gaps between the words.

'What's big enough to bite off the body of a hundred-pound shark?' He didn't look at anyone and he didn't expect an answer.

'Packy, Joby,' he added rapidly, his voice louder. 'Start the engine. We're going in.'

The Goat clutched his flask, blood fleeing his face. Jack stood still. I was about to cry. Father looked out over the rolling sea and said just two words, slowly, deliberately, as if talking to himself – *killer whale*.

We had a name for it. The Donovans rushed to the motor as Father swung the shark head into the boat, kicking aside the bundle of lines, reels, hooks and floats. Jack and I retreated to the cabin door, out of the way. We left room for The Goat who huddled close to us and started to drink. But just as he held the flask to his mouth, the boat jerked down at the back, sending whiskey shooting through his teeth.

'We're taking water!' The Goat wailed. For a split second

the stern of the two-ton trawler dipped towards the swell, before springing back level again. Lines of wavelets rushed out from the hull as it listed back and forth, a sea cradle rocked by some underwater hand. Big Jim ran to the stern, looked over.

'The rubby-dubby!' he shouted. 'The bastard has bitten the lot!'

I smelled iodine at the back of my nose.

Before any of us could move, the killer struck again, more resolute this time. Its white belly was right beneath us now, a gross white mass brushing gently against the keel, toying with us, raising us as it lay on its back, an oversized freak in some horrible circus act.

'Hold steady,' Big Jim said. 'No one's to panic. Stay as you are.'

Father held Jack and me tight. Jack stood firm, but I wept huge gobs of tears.

Big Jim jacked the engine and spun the wheel full circle. *The Ballycotton Star* spat back to life, lurching forward in a cloud of smoke. And as we all stood motionless, Father lifted the camera from Jack's shoulder and pointed it towards the stern. Just in time to catch the black tail of the killer rise up behind us, like a monster doing a handstand under water, spread out in a still pose, before diving down in a thunderclap of surf.

Gulls hovered above us as we motored in, screeching and screaming for scraps of fish bait left over from the rubby-dubby. Looking up at one flock crossing our bows, Big Jim quizzed his sons. Gannets? Guillemots? Petrels? Puffins? Razorbills? Joby and Packy didn't seem to know and Big Jim didn't say. But he did tell the story about birds making letters in the sky when they flew; and if they were cranes, he said lifting an eyebrow, they sometimes carried a sack made from the skin of a woman, a bag full of secret words stolen from the king of the sea. When the tide was high the letters could be read through the water; when low the bag was empty!

'Now full, now empty.' Jack echoed Big Jim's riddle. 'Just like the rubby-dubby.'

When we reached Ballycotton port, we went for a drink in Lane's pub. Father bought hot toddies while Jack and I retold what happened, over and over. We passed the photo round and several people in the pub came to look. Jack asked Father if he could keep it, and Father, putting his hand on Jack's head, said yes.

I knew where Jack would keep it. In the secret box under his bed-table with his silver christening pen and Kennedy stamps. That's where Jack put it; and that's where I took it from and hid it away where no one could find it, even though Jack fretted and Mother had us all search the house. No one found it and every so often, after that, I would take it out and look at it. Father's photograph. Jack's photograph. My photograph.

Entry 5
Christian Brothers Cork, May 1962

'You are ready. You are now ready, boys, to become vessels of the Word.' Brother Keogh was speaking, promising us that the Son of God would soon be a *real presence* inside us. Then we'd be 'guided and sheltered' by Jesus, hidden in the 'waters streaming from his side', just like the Communion song said. But first, the Canon's exam. We'd recite the Beatitudes one last time before he arrived.

Brother Keogh was a Christian Brother. A short man with funny eyes, sometimes grey, sometimes blue. He had a small mouth, but was a great talker. He called Jack and me 'the Toland two-oh', and said if we did our lessons exactly as he asked, we'd be as bright as the Kennedy brothers in Washington, when we grew up. He was always going on about Jack being short for John. John F. Kennedy to the political electorate, Jack Kennedy to family and friends. My Jack thought that was a laugh. I thought it was silly.

Our school was called Christian Brothers Cork, CBC for short; or sometimes just plain Christians. It ran from Wellington Road called after a British general, to McCurtain, called after a Republican martyr. There were other Christian Brothers schools in Cork. But they didn't play rugby. Jack was a brilliant rugby player. I'd cheer him on with the crowd, chanting the old CBC anthem:

> evan, iven, ee-zoh-zum
> we're the boys who drink no rum
> rum-rum-rummy-rummy-rum-rum-rum-rum

I didn't have the foggiest what that meant; neither did Jack. I'm not sure we were meant to. But it sounded great.

CBC's big enemy was PBC – Presentation Brothers College, Pres for short. It was on the other side of town, further up the river near the Mardyke, and the only other school in Cork that played rugby. The cup match every year was like a faction fight. But I didn't understand how schools run by 'Brothers' could hate each other so much. Pres colours were black and white; ours were black, yellow and red. Both of us had 'Internationals'. Tommy Kiernan, who kicked over a hundred goals for Ireland, was theirs. Noel Murphy, who was knocked out by a Welsh forward for trying to bite off his earlobe, was ours. Brother Keogh said Jack could be as good as either of them if he practised enough.

Canon Warren was due any minute, and we were still rehearsing catechism answers Brother Keogh had drilled into us over the year. Most of us had them by heart by now, even the words we didn't understand. *Calumny, presumption, covetousness, concupiscence.* We'd say them to ourselves so often they were part of us. Like the words we learned for Mass. *Laetificat, iuventutem, seculorum, spiritu.* Special kinds of sounds, repeated again and again, for special times. Sounds we didn't hear every day. Like Jack's secret.

Brother Keogh was jittery that day. Almost sixty, he paced up and down the class as if he was getting ready for the hundred yards. His black soutane was shiny under the elbows when he lifted his arms, the front a Milky Way of chalk dust which he covered himself with every time he cleaned the board with a duster. We loved it when he did that; and when he told us stories from the Bible. Especially when he told them in his own words and images. Adam and Eve talking with thick Cork accents or Moses walking down Oliver Plunkett Street with eyes peeled for Egyptians. His ramblings floated over us like flotsam on a neap tide. Jack and I revelled in them, though we rarely remembered what they were examples of. Except when they were about brothers. Abel and Cain we remembered, and Moses and Aaron, Tobias and Raphael, Joseph and Benjamin, Jacob and Esau. The last was our favourite. And we'd often retell it to each other, just as Brother Keogh told it, until we knew it off by heart.

It began with a lady called Rebecca who had two babies in her womb. The first-born, all covered in red hair, was Esau. The next, born still grabbing his brother's heel, was Jacob. In the Jewish language, *Jacob* means someone who catches another's foot, trips him up, takes his place, cheats. That's what Brother Keogh said. The hairy Esau was always out hunting and became his father's favourite. Jacob stayed in the tents with his mother and dreamed. Until he stole the blessing. Dressed in Esau's animal skins, Jacob pretended he was his brother. And his father, Isaac, old and blind, believed him and gave him the blessing. When Esau returned from the hunt he discovered that Jacob had taken his 'birthright'. He wanted to kill him but Jacob escaped to Haran, in the East, where his mother's family lived. On the way there Jacob had a dream (our favourite bit) about a huge ladder reaching from the ground up to heaven with angels going up and down. And while he dreamed of angels, God came close and whispered in his ear that he would one day find a land of milk and honey. After the dream, Jacob went to his uncle's house where he fell in love with his cousin Rachel. He kissed her for the first time beside a well where her flocks were drinking. After fourteen years an angel came to tell Jacob to come home to the land of Esau. So he put his family on camels and travelled back to his brother's land; and when he reached the River Jordan he was met by a company of angels who told him to divide everything in two before crossing. He did and slept on his own and wrestled with an angel all through the night. He was struck on the hip but he would not let that angel go until it gave its blessing. And because he didn't give up he saw the face of the Lord and received the secret name of *Israel*, meaning the *one who wrestled with the Lord*. Next day, Jacob crossed the river and was reconciled with Esau. But we never knew if he told him the secret.

Every time we retold this story, Jack would crack the joke about Jacob's fig roll biscuits. *Question: How did Jacob get the figs into the fig rolls? Answer: E-saw how to do it in a dream!* Jack knew lots of things like that. But the best thing he knew was the 'secret'.

There was a scuffle in the classroom then. The Canon was arriving. Almost twelve o'clock. Our class huddled into two rows as he entered. He was wearing a black suit and flat cap – we were hoping for purple robes and a shining mitre. He blessed us with a sweeping wave of his hand and chatted to Brother Keogh, until the clock chimed and we all made the sign of the Cross. The Angelus.

Brother Keogh and the Canon faced the crucifix on the front wall. We knelt behind them, heads bent, reciting together the words of the prayer. The angel asking Mary and Mary saying yes. Surely this was the time to try out the 'secret', I thought. So I undid my trousers and, without letting anyone see, took out my penis. My eyes closed as I pulled it back and forth, the prayer getting quicker, phrase by phrase, until I came to the final bit, my heart louder than the words now, hoping the feeling would come all in a rush just when Mary answered the angel.

It was Jack who first told me the secret. He said it was the Protestant boy staying in the chalet beside us at Myrtleville told him, and that it was really easy and you felt great if you did it long enough. He said it was a special secret and that I should tell no one else. The first few times I tried it nothing happened. But Jack said to keep on trying and one day I'd know the secret feeling – *the feeling of angels*.

He was right. It did work at last, one evening as I was kneeling by my bed to say my nighttime prayer:

> O angel of God, my guardian dear,
> to whom God's love commits me here,
> ever this day be at my side,
> to light and guard, to rule and guide,
> and if I die before I wake,
> I give to you my soul to take.

It was while saying these words over and over, as I did the secret thing and imagined the angel lifting its hair up at the neck, that it eventually happened, coming through me in one glorious rush. My heart tumbled inside me. *The feeling of angels*, I said to myself. Jack was right. It *was* the feeling of angels.

When I told Jack it had worked at last, he told me more. He said this was the feeling that made each of us the 'image and likeness' of God, like in the catechism, and that it was only because believing in Jesus and Mary made you feel like this that so many people all over the world were Christians, even in Africa and Australia. Did Protestants feel like that too? I asked, and Jack reminded me it was the Protestant boy who told him the secret in the first place. And Jews? Of course: wasn't Mary a Jew like Joseph and Jesus? So Jesus felt it too? Jesus felt it more than anyone, Jack said. Jesus had *twice* the feeling of angels; and not just that, he had it *all the time*!

One thing still puzzled me though. Why did no one speak about this wonder of religion? Why had Brother Keogh never mentioned it? Why did it have to be secret? Maybe we'd have to wait for First Communion to be told? Maybe it was being kept to the end, like all good things? Maybe Brother Keogh was so taken by the other stories that he actually forgot the best one of all?

Jack had no idea. But he was able to tell me what the feeling of angels had to do with Holy Communion. Judas, he explained, was so jealous of Jesus's secret feeling that he told the Roman soldiers who crucified him on the Cross. And it was because Judas passed over to the other side that the Jews call Easter *pass over*, the time of the Last Supper, the time of Holy Communion. And it was three days after that, after the supper and the sacrifice, that the body of Jesus rose from the tomb. The Word was made flesh again and the feeling of angels returned to the world. That's why Mary Magdalene first saw Jesus walking from the grave in the form of an angel. And that's why Holy Communion is a time when the angel passes over and back between man and God making Jesus *really present* once more. Like the angels moving up and down Jacob's ladder.

Wasn't it only right, then, I thought to myself, to have the feeling of angels on Communion day? Wasn't it right that, after all the talk about words becoming flesh, the words of the Angelus should come at the same time as the rush of angel feeling? *Verbum caro factum est.* Wasn't that Jack's secret too?

My eyes opened to see the Canon looking at me.

'What is the meaning of this?' he asked.

'It's the feeling of angels . . .' I said, pleased to share the secret at last.

The Canon waved me to one side of the class, and I stood there staring up at him. His skin was creamy pale in the light streaming in from the grimy panes, his eyes lidless – gull-eyes. I felt like a small silent fish pouting gills against the side of a great glass tank. The Canon asked more questions then, his voice softer, more solicitous.

'What is this feeling of angels, my child?'

'It's Jack's secret, Your Grace.'

'And who is Jack?'

'My brother.'

'And what does Jack say?'

I glanced at Jack at the back of the class but couldn't catch his eye. I waited for a second, my lips moving in silence, but thought it must be all right to say it to a Canon. He couldn't be that close to God and *not* know. I'd only be telling him what he already knew. Like reciting an answer from the catechism book. Jack wouldn't mind that, would he?

'The feeling of angels is what Gabriel felt when he asked Mary to have God's son and what Mary felt when she said yes . . .'

The Canon still didn't seem to understand, so I tried to explain it better.

'Gabriel felt it because he was an angel; Mary felt it because she was perfect and had perfect feelings; and Jesus felt it *twice* as much as anyone else and felt it *all the time* . . .'

The Canon of Cork was right above me now. He smelled of sweet soap. But he wasn't looking at me any more. He was looking straight at Jack, standing at the back of the class.

'Do you realize, child, the wrong you've done?' he asked Jack. Jack said nothing. The Canon's face flamed up, then paled again, the skin clinging tight to his bones. Fear gagged my soul as I watched. I knew it wasn't over yet. Something passed across the emptiness between us, like wings brushing, as Jack's voice rose up boldly from his place at the end of the room. 'It can't be wrong, Your Grace. It *is* the feeling of angels . . .'

The Canon said nothing more to Jack. He simply motioned him to stand to the other side of the room and proceeded to call the rest of us forward, one by one, to answer questions from the catechism book. We all passed. Even me. Every one of us, except Jack. But I knew the angel was on Jack's side.

Entry 6
Cork, October 1962

Flah-bag, Cork-screw, Nanny-fanny. Some of the names we called her. Her real name was Nurse Tuama, but we never called her that. She was nice to grown-ups, terrible to us. She had big white hands which got bigger every time she came to stay, and eyes like a herring's, always open, with a tawny cast in the middle. She had a bun too, tied up in a cobweb net at the back of her head.

This time, Jack said, it was time to fight back. Our parents had hardly been away on holiday a day when Jack made a plan. We began by giving new names to bits of the house and garden. We called the basement *Glassie Alley*; the hot-press *Hadji Bey's*; the lower garden *Desert Bluff*; the path behind the trees *Gurriers Glen*. Nurse Tuama wouldn't have an idea what we were talking about. We also made up lots of passwords – *glicout, mariyah, goosah, shoneen, doodenah* and *gottenhimmel*. Words we overheard from gangs on our way home from school or from the sailor boys below in Lovers Walk.

We did whatever Nurse Tuama said, of course. Nothing left on our plates, baths before seven, bed before eight. But as soon as we were alone, we worked on the plot. We took our name from *The Hardy Boys*, our favourite book, then serialized on pirate radio. The Hardy brothers were the kind of guys who kept their nerve like JFK during the Missile Crisis and had no fear of Cubans or Koreans. Far braver than the Holy Joe heroes of our CBC magazine, *Our Boys*. Jack and I took it in turns to read each other chapters, saying the lines in a long, low whisper even when there was no one else around. The more we read about the two Hardy brothers the more we *became* them. Who was more real? Them or us? It didn't matter. What mattered was we knew their words by heart and could pass in and out of their world. A game between the four of us. Closer than blood brothers. Book brothers.

Passing by the landing one day, Nurse Tuama overheard us pretending to be Frank and Joe Hardy plotting her death with made-up walkie-talkies: *Come in, Roger! Come in, Roger! Do you read me? Do you read me? Flah-bag is an enemy agent! Fight to the death! Over!* She pulled open the door and threatened to wash our tongues out with soap. But she settled for less – making us stay in the next day, a Saturday and free day from school.

Jack decided it was time to act. The first stage of the plan was codes. We started by making different letters of the alphabet stand for one another – A for O, I for E, U for N, L for T, and so on. But that was too difficult and we kept getting mixed up. So Jack thought of a better way: the Hardy Boys' trick of writing words backwards to make a secret message. To read it afterwards you just held it before a mirror and the words turned back the right way again. As Jack was confined to the drawing room, I to the bedroom, he wrote the message and left it behind the pipe in the upstairs bathroom for me to collect. The signal was three short flushes. But just after I heard it and was about to open my bedroom door, Nurse Tuama walked by the landing. I was nearly found out. I stayed put for a few minutes until I was sure she'd gone. When I got to the lavatory the note was still there, written in bold strokes, looped and laced and, most important of all, *backwards*. Back in my bedroom I held it to the mirror and the writing unfolded in front of me in a magic switch of letters:

TOP SECRET. DEAR HARDY BROTHER. FLAH-BAG THE EVIL OCCUPIER MUST BE PUT AWAY BEFORE SHE COMMITS MORE DOODENAH CRIMES. SECRET MEETING TO BE HELD IN DESERT BLUFF. ESCAPE PLAN – SNEAK OUT GLASSIE ALLEY DOOR AT SIX WHEN FLAH-BAG IS LISTENING TO NEWS. MARIYAH AND GOTTENHIMMEL. YOUR HARDY BROTHER.

It was already six when I met up with Jack by the basement door. Just like the message said. We could hear the Angelus chiming away on the upstairs radio as we lifted the latch. But someone was there before us. Standing right outside the door. Nurse Tuama. And she was holding Mother's riding whip.

'Just where are you two off to?' she asked.

'We're going to Mrs Furlong's to do messages,' said Jack.

'And who asked you to do messages?'

'Big Nora,' Jack said.

'Is that true?' Nurse Tuama turned to Big Nora the maid, whose huge frame was puffing in from the kitchen to see what was up.

'No,' said Big Nora. Her wide mouth was beaming.

'So you're two little liars into the bargain!' said Nurse Tuama.

'We just want to go for a walk. We've been in all day. We'll tell our parents when they come back.' Jack did all the talking. I didn't say a word. Big Nora was delighted and mocked away at us with her little rhyme.

> Tell-tale tit, your tongues shall be slit,
> and all the doggies in the town
> will eat a little bit!

But Nurse Tuama was in no mood for foolery.

'You'll both run off to France and tell your parents you're two little liars, will you now?'

'We will if we have to,' Jack replied.

'That's where you're off to now then, is it, France?'

'No.'

'Where are you off to so?'

'Nowhere.'

'Is *Desert Bluff* nowhere?'

'No . . .'

'And what are you going to do there?'

'Nothing . . .'

'Is *putting Flah-bag away* nothing?'

The game was up. Nurse Tuama had read the note. She'd cracked the code.

'If you apologize there will be no punishment,' she promised, the riding whip held down by her side.

Jack ran to the back of the basement and grabbed two pieces of Father's fibreglass fishing rod. He kept one, threw me the other.

'It's a fight to the finish so.' Big Nora giggled, all thirteen stone of her weaving up and down.

'Put away those rods and I'll put down the whip,' said Nurse Tuama. Jack looked at me and shook his head. I knew he was right. But something in me had to *believe*.

'Cross your heart and hope to die?' I asked Nurse Tuama.

'Don't!' Jack shouted to me.

'Promise?' I asked again, handing her my rod.

The nails on her big hands were moonless, all eaten away at the tips, I noticed, as she struck again and again. And at each stroke, I felt a sharp knot of wrong twist within my chest. When it came to Jack's turn, tears rushed into his eyes, only to be beaten back.

I went to the sitting room after, and turned on Father's radio. I moved the knob from left to right and listened to foreign voices wash over me, one more incomprehensible than the next.

Entry 7
Cork, November 1963

Wednesday afternoons, Jack and I would wait at our bedroom window for Maggie and Veronica Kiely to arrive. They were our favourite cousins and the sight of their faces on the garden path made our hearts loud. Wednesday was our half-day from school, the day the four of us met to play Rude Doctors.

Our mother and their mother were sisters-in-law. They were best friends growing up and went to the same school and were always helping each other out, exchanging clothes and magazines and stories, and children. But that didn't stop Jack and me teasing the Kiely girls with the rhyme about the bleeding mothers:

> My mother and your mother
> were hanging out the clothes,
> my mother gave your mother
> a punch on the nose
> what colour was the blood?
>
> Red?
>
> R-E-D spells red
> and out of this game
> you shall go
> with a jolly good punch
> on the nose.

Maggie and Veronica replied with the ink rhyme:

> A bottle of ink fell down the sink
> How many inches did it sink?
>
> Ten?
>
> T-E-N spells ten
> and out of this game
> you shall go
> whether you like it
> or no.

None of us knew what blood had to do with ink, but it didn't matter.

Veronica was eleven and loved trying on make-up and clothes. Maggie was nine – same as me and Jack. We both liked Maggie best, though she liked Jack better than me. She was a tomboy, hated dresses and hardly ever cried. She'd raise her eyes to heaven whenever she didn't understand something or thought something was stupid.

We lived in each other's houses. This wasn't hard as we lived at different ends of the same road. The road didn't have a name but their end was called Montenotte and ours Tivoli. Italian names, Mother said, though no Italians lived there. The road was like a line running through the hill, connecting our side to theirs. We were always running over and back. That was fine, our mothers said, as long as we didn't cross the line, up or down. If we wandered up towards Mayfield we'd cross a path where high trees threw black shadows and a bearded man dressed as a nun once raped a girl and strangled her with rosary beads (that's what Big Nora told us). If we wandered down, past Lovers Walk or Corkscrew Hill, we'd come upon a lane descending to the docks below where, after dark, fat girls with make-up used to ride with foreign sailors up against the high walls, leaving behind them stained hankies which the dogs carried back to their Montenotte homes.

Rude Doctors was simple at first. The consulting room, as Jack called it, was the hot-press on the third floor of our house. It was warm and dark with lots of cotton sheets, towels and underwear: just the place for Maggie and Veronica to take their clothes off, lie down, close their eyes and show off what they called their secret wounds. Jack and I would examine them with Father's old eye-torch and glasses – the special ones for his glaucoma patients. *Joey Eyes* was our father's nickname, and that's what Jack insisted I call him whenever we played Doctors. Jack was always the house surgeon, I was the ambulance man, Veronica the matron, Maggie the nurse.

Jack would make me wait outside the hot-press with my pretend stretcher while he was 'operating' inside. He'd say he could only cure one lady patient at a time, usually Maggie, as she never minded taking all her clothes off. And Veronica and I would get so fed up listening to their whispers and giggles we'd sometimes wander into the nearby loo and kiss with tight mouths until we could hardly breathe. She wouldn't ever open her lips. She said I was too young. Maggie opened her lips all right, but she was always with Jack. And they took ages. We played Rude Doctors at the Kielys' house too. They had a big basement with huge flat stones, washing lines hanging from the ceiling and rows upon rows of wooden shelves storing cooking apples from the garden, whose sweet smell mixed with that of the soap from the drying sheets to make a special underground odour. Sometimes there was a tart smell that hit the back of the nose and eyes, if you passed near the rotting brown tails of the onions on the bottom shelves. The big difference when we played at the Kielys' though was that Maggie and Veronica wanted to do the operating and Jack and I had to lie down and be patients. If we refused, Veronica would make us do dares, like drinking a jam-jar full of smelly yellow medicine, putting our bums out of the window as cars passed by, or crawling between the legs of Lizzie the maid to see if the hair on her legs went all the way up to her knickers.

After a while we began to fight so much over which house we'd play in, Jack suggested we move our consulting rooms somewhere new, somewhere we'd never been before, somewhere – why not? – beyond the line of safety. We settled on the old abandoned garage below Lovers Walk.

We knew we were doing wrong and we didn't care. We had been warned, of course, lots of times. And not just by our mothers, but by things we'd seen with our own eyes. Late on summer evenings, a noisy gang from the Mayfield estates roamed down on to our road, catapults in hand. 'Goodie-goodie gobshites!' they'd cat-call after us. 'Proddy-woddy wankers!', even though hardly any Protestants lived on our road any more.

The Mayfield Gang. The sound of the name made our

palms wet. They hung out in a pub for fellows on the dole called the Fox and Hounds. Their leader was Cormac O'Keefe, expelled from school at the age of twelve for assaulting one of his teachers and notorious for torturing pet spaniels and pure-bred cats, smashing car windows after nightfall and calling after prostitutes and their foreign sailor boys. We'd often hear Big Nora and Lizzie go on about them. *Gurriers* and *Gutties*, they called them, scaring the daylights out of us.

The day we moved our pretend 'rooms' down through the gardens of lavender and lilac to the garage beneath Lovers Walk, we smelt something sharper in the air. We were leaving the row of high-walled three-storey houses behind us and stepping into dockland – the place where angry-looking men from the quays laboured, where seamen and lipsticked ladies did things to each other, where gurriers and gutties met and cursed. The high view over the River Lee, stretching from the Marina Boat Club out to Blackrock Castle, was disappearing fast, and we could no longer even see the funnels of the cargo ships steaming in from Portsmouth, Plymouth or Fishguard. The old garage lay at the very bottom of the hill, the narrow road leading down to it like the gullet of a sprawling animal. It was one of the last days of November, I remember, the same week as President Kennedy was shot in Dallas.

The garage was full of broken boxes with a rusty model-T Ford sitting in one of its corners. It was all dark inside. Jack, who had a toy collection of vintage cars, was delighted. But before he got a chance to have a proper look, someone stepped towards us from the back of the garage. We knew, before he told us, who he was. Cormac O'Keefe. He had a teddy-boy quiff and made a purring sound with his tongue as he sidled up to Veronica, stroking her fawn hair. She wasn't afraid. None of us were. Cormac O'Keefe made us laugh. He had smiley eyes.

He told us how he fooled the 'Holy fucking Joes' at school before they kicked him out. He used words we'd never heard before – *langer, fuckpuss, gobblejob, sweatie, bogah, shitehawk*. They rolled off his tongue, sing-song quick, and we knew they had a special power. They came from somewhere we had never been. When we asked him what they meant, he said they were the Facts of Life. Did we want to know the Facts of Life? he asked.

Cormac O'Keefe looked about him for a moment just then, before climbing on to the front seat of the Ford. He had us form a queue. When each of our turns came, he said, we were to open the door, and sit in the back. 'Like First Confession,' Jack said, going in first. He came out white. Veronica was next, then Maggie, wrinkling up her nose and raising her brown eyes to heaven. My turn at last. I opened the rusty handle, sat on the soft, peeling leather and waited for the voice. There was a smell of Woodbine cigarettes and Brylcreem.

'You want to know the Facts of Life?' he said.

'Yes,' I said.

'It's simple. The man takes out his langer and shoves it up the lady's sweatie. If the lady's sweatie is bleeding when he does it, she has a baby. If it's not bleeding, she doesn't. If the man gives her a gobble job she might have twins. And if he does it in the bogah, she won't have anything. You see?'

'I see,' I said.

We ran all the way home, Maggie and Veronica to their house, Jack and I to ours. Inside, Jack went straight to the drawing room and turned on the radio. I sat beside him for a while as we listened to the high, run-away voice of Michael O hEithir doing the races from the Curragh. One race followed another, words passing over our heads, quicker than the horses they were naming, images flashing fast as the wind, hearts still leaping in our ribs. But the panic did not go away. Finally Jack suggested we tell Mother, everything, even if she scolded us for crossing the line, for going down to that place. We had to know if it was true and Mother wouldn't lie.

We went upstairs to her bedroom. It was the middle of the afternoon, her rest-time. She wasn't asleep. We could hear a voice inside. At first we thought there was someone with her. But there wasn't, she was just talking on the telephone. Her voice was happy, pausing in between each sentence. We knocked.

'Who is it?'

'It's Sam and me,' said Jack. 'We need to ask you something.'

'Can't it wait?'

'No.'

'Until tea-time?'

'No, it must be now.'

'Come in, then.'

We went in. It was the first time we'd been into her room during rest-time. She was lying up on her bed, shoes and stockings off, one hand over the phone. Her eyes were kind and deep. Smiley eyes. I hadn't ever noticed before.

'What is it, my loves?' she said, replacing the receiver.

Jack repeated word for word what Cormac O'Keefe had just told us. 'Is it true?' he asked.

She didn't say a thing at first. Her eyes became a little wet, that's all, and she looked away, staring at her blue and white hyacinths on the bedside table for what seemed like ages. Her face seemed to change colour, ever so slightly, more pale and then more dark. When she did speak, after a long while, she just said, 'People only do that when they love each other very much.' Then, her voice so quiet we could barely hear, 'And those are not the words for it. They are not the words. Believe me.'

We wanted to believe her but we couldn't. There was love, oh, so much love in every phrase but it was not enough.

'Cormac O'Keefe is right,' Jack said and left the room.

I waited behind a moment, for something to happen, anything, another phrase, a light in her eyes, a movement of her hand that would put everything back as it was. But there were no more words, and her eyes didn't brighten, and her hand didn't move towards me. No, her hand just turned her small earrings, seed-pearls, round and round the base of her ear.

Entry 8
Myrtleville, July 1964

We fancied the same babysitter. She looked after us when we were small, during summer holidays in the chalet in Myrtleville whenever our parents drove back to Cork city – Father to see his patients in Sydney Parade, Mother to shop in Patrick's Street. Mary Murphy was a local girl, from Myrtleville village. She was a brick, Mother used to say. Reliable, solid, great grip. Jack and I thought she was gorgeous. We were ten when she came to work for us; she was fifteen:

Mary Murphy loved boats, with a passion. Though she always stayed in the same room as Jack and me whenever she stayed overnight, something in her always stayed away. She often had that stray look, especially when she'd gaze out to sea. Maybe she was originally from the sea, Jack used to say, like one of those siren ladies she read to us about at bedtime. Maybe that was why she smelt like the sea if you crept into her bed early in the morning when she was still asleep. We'd often do that, and it was true, she

did have a seaweedy smell. Like iodine for grazed knees –
a deep-sea smell.

Anyway, Mary Murphy loved boats and was always
telling stories about them. Usually about shipwrecked ones,
lost at sea, or hit by lightning in the middle of storms.
She'd rush to the windows of the chalet as soon as a sail
or steamship appeared on the horizon. And she'd get even
more excited when the ocean liners glided past the Daunt
Rock lightship on their passage from Cobh to America.
They were the special treat. She'd stand on her tiptoes
to see over the tops of the red fuchsia bushes, trying to
make out the lettering on the giant distant prows. Then
she'd lift me and Jack up, one after the other, so we could
see too. We had great fun making out the long names.
Mauritania. Queen Elizabeth. Queen Mary – her favourite,
of course. These transatlantic steamers, she'd tell us in
deliberate words, were now passing over the remains of
their former sister ship, The *Lusitania*, sunk by a German
U-Boat in the First World War with hundreds of women
and children drowned. We knew that one by heart: our
best bedtime story every summer. Mary Murphy gave each
detail of bravery and pain. Especially the bit about the grand
English lady floating in her huge white petticoats grasping
two small children in her arms.

Most nights, after the story and prayers, she'd turn on a
transistor and let us go to sleep listening to Radio Caroline.
Mary Murphy said the voices were broadcast from a boat
miles out at sea.

Most of Mary Murphy's family – brothers, sisters, uncles,
cousins – had made the journey from Cobh to New York;
and the first thing they did on arrival was to send home
postcards of the ocean liner that had taken them. Mary
had a great collection. She kept them beside her row
of holy pictures – Virgin Marys and saints: Our Lady
of Fatima, Our Lady of Lourdes, Saint Theresa of the

Little Flowers, Saint Theresa of Avila, Saint Catherine of Siena. All bluey-green, all aquamarine, holy colours, her favourite colours. And whenever we'd recite the Hail Holy Queen with her before going to bed at night or sing her favourite hymn – O Mary we crown thee with blossoms today, Queen of the Angels and Queen of the May – we'd look up at those pictures pinned over the bed. Words and images magically mixed. Queen Mary. Queen of the May. Mother of God and Ocean Liner. She had a lot to live up to, Mary Murphy, and she was proud of it.

But Mary Murphy had a special passion for little boats. Like the ones moored below in the cove at Myrtleville, the place the locals still called by its Irish name – Poul Gorm. *Poul* meaning hole or gap. *Gorm* meaning sea-blue, ink-blue, the colour of deep water. Mary sat there on the stones as she minded us playing by the water or picking away at the cracked bits of paint on the fishing punts pulled up on the stones, breathing in the smell of fresh bubbled tar daubed over the wooden hulls for the summer's fishing. She'd often gaze across to Ringabella beach at the other end of the bay, or just straight out to sea. One time, she was so distracted she didn't notice me undo a mooring rope and push Jack out on one of the small boats. A man swimming nearby retrieved him before he'd got far. When Mary scolded me, I said Jack should be allowed to go to America too if he wanted to. Like all her brothers.

One morning I woke Mary Murphy early. I whispered so as not to wake Jack, still asleep beside her in the bed. I asked her to come down and watch me have a swim before breakfast. She agreed, still sleepy, with that deep-sea smell. She didn't make me wake Jack. She knew I didn't want to.

Down at Poul Gorm, that morning, everything was blue and white. Water colours, like one of mother's aquarelles. It was as if the sea was saying the word, under its breath

– aquarelle – the word that sounded like a woman's name, like watery ink seeping through paper, inviting us under its moving skin. Heat was rising off the stones in a haze, unusual so early in the morning, with nobody else down yet for a dip. Only me and Mary Murphy. The two of us.

There was a small fishing boat tied off the south rock. A white rowing punt with a tiny rolled gibsail. I dived in and swam towards it. I was a strong swimmer for ten. Mary sat on the rock and looked on, wavering a little in the sea haze. I climbed dripping into the boat. Mary called out: she wanted me to bring the boat into shore so she could get in, just for a minute. She wanted me to take a photo of her with the camera she'd brought. Just this once. She'd send copies to her cousins in New York, she said.

Why not? My chance to do something for Mary that Jack could not do. My own prize photo, specially for Mary. (Better than a whale.) I pulled the mooring rope until the punt reached Mary on the rocks. She got in and handed me the camera as I clambered on to the shore. I pushed the bow firmly, waved pretend-goodbye and brought the camera into focus – just in time to see Mary, through the framed lens, stand up, wave back and slip. She disappeared.

The splash was followed by flat calm, the sea haze still the same, the gulls' crying as before. Mary Murphy couldn't swim. I jumped in and struggled towards the boat, arms and legs kicking wildly. I dived down at the spot where she'd vanished – and there she was, her face right before mine now, like when she woke early in the morning to find me beside her. But her arms reached out to circle me now like they never did in the morning. And her eyes were wide open now, even under water, like they never were in the morning. And there was no smell, under water, and no sound. Only bubbles, huge white bubbles, billowing up from her blue mouth, like gibsails in a squall. I wished Jack was with me now. He'd save her.

I pushed her away; as firmly as I'd pushed the little boat out from the rock. I rose to the surface and sucked in air. I swam ashore, like a chased animal, and left her there. I left her, lying silently, all by herself, under that little capsized fishing boat in Myrtleville, in Poul Gorm, sea haze blurring the line between sky and sea, water colours, bluey-green.

*

Jack pushes the chair back from Sam's desk. He gets up and reaches across for a glass which he fills with cold water from the basin tap beside Sam's bed. Then he walks to the window, slowly, his feet moving forward one by one as if responding to some invisible pull. He opens the window and stares into the night. The cool air brings him back to himself.

Sam had never said a word. He was there when Mary Murphy drowned and he never told anyone. He must have sneaked back up to bed, pretending to be asleep when Mother came to wake them with the news that the body had been washed up in Poul Gorm. Sam had cried along with Jack and never said a thing. And the camera? What did he do with the camera?

Was it from guilt Sam cried so inconsolably that morning? From the shock of seeing her die? From fear of being found out? Jack's face fills with puzzlement. Some doubt niggles him. Maybe Sam wasn't there. Maybe he had made it up to fit some narrative plot. To explain his first rupture of desire, the terrifying loss, the opening of an unfathomable gap which in time would lead inevitably to his withdrawal from this world. A groove cut deep in the field of his soul. A first step dug on his way to God.

Was it just a twist of fiction, then, to help Sam make some sense of himself? Another coy deception, like stealing the photo of the whale or the picture of the horse. Even the fragments of whimsical anecdote – Nurse Tuama, Cormac O'Keefe, the 'feeling of angels' – even they were full of mutiple inaccuracies. Irrelevant, scarcely noticeable, but striking for Jack nonetheless, almost irritating. Nurse had never beaten Sam with Father's rod. Mother was never told of how they'd learned the 'facts of life'. Brother Keogh, not the Canon, was the one to discover the 'secret of angels' in Communion class.

But why would Sam want to change things around like that? Jack stands upright, jiggling the remaining water in his glass. He continues to gaze out of the window into the dark. Was it to impress Anselm with a sequence of childhood events prefiguring his calling? Was it to hide a bigger lie with little lies? Some harmless addiction to fantasy? Or did Sam actually believe he was telling the truth?

Jack brings a hand to his forehead and draws it back through his dark red hair. He rubs his eyes. He is, he realizes, becoming more confused. Just now, in fact, Jack wishes for one thing – to talk to Sam. To check their versions of the way things really happened. To verify a common past. But it's too late for that now. Two days too late. If only they had talked before Sam died, but they had not. And Jack weeps now, for himself, for Sam, for something lost and unrecoverable.

For a brief minute the forest surrounding the Abbey is lit up by the moon passing between clouds. The blurred dark horizon crystallizes into sharp outlines and shapes, and Jack imagines he can tell one type of tree from another. The names come back to him, one by one. The names he'd learned from Anselm as a boarder in the Abbey. Montezuma pines. Sierra redwoods. European larches. Cherry laurels. White magnolias. Ilchester oaks.

Jack mouths the names to himself without quite knowing why. He finishes the glass of water, closes the window, and returns to the open journal on Sam's desk.

THE LIFE OF TOBIAS

PART TWO

'With various lusts laid aside and with the causes of disagreement and difference cut off, all the sons of God shall mutually enjoy themselves a true peace and entire charity, by the likeness of their characters and the agreement of their single will. For great harm is done by difference of character and diversity of practice . . . Let us hasten to heal the poisons of envy and vain glory through the teaching of our Saviour who says: Let us all, made perfect with no further blemish, with hatred rooted out, love one another with our whole heart.'

The Works of St Columbanus, Epistula II, 5. AD 603

∫

There were two leaders of our Tivoli gang. There was Jack
and there was Jer McCarthy, a boy from the B class in school
whom Jack decided one day was his best friend. Jer wasn't
a nice person. He was a person who hated nice people. He
preferred Cromwell to Patrick Sarsfield, Eamon de Valera
to Michael Collins, Lee Harvey Oswald to John Fitzgerald
Kennedy.

Jack didn't seem to mind, even if JFK was his best dead
hero. He'd egg Jer on, laughing more the worse he became.
It wasn't that hard for Jer to play the bad guy as he was
fiercely ugly. His neck was so short you'd think his head
had been stuck straight on to his body like one of those
put-together plastic soldiers; his eyes were flat and stony,
like a lizard's. But Jer didn't seem to mind. He could do
all sorts of things we couldn't, like make the sound of a
train by moving his tongue from one cheek to the other,
sucking air in and out, or hoot like an owl by cupping
his two hands to his mouth and blowing through a tiny
gap between his thumbs. He could also light fires with a
spectacle lens, build traps for magpies, and recite the Top
Ten from Radio Luxembourg.

Jer was also the strongest of the gang. He beat Jack and me at hand wrestling every time, lying flat on his tummy with his left arm locked in mine, his right in Jack's, pulling us both into a single grip of squeezed hands. He'd smile then, a sidelong smile, as if he were impressing some invisible onlooker. Jer was street-wise. He'd been brought up on gangster stories by his five older brothers while his dad was off in the Congo fighting Balubas with the Irish Army. His dad was a private and didn't earn much money. Jer never had a penny on him and the hallway of his flat down by St Luke's Cross was nearly always dark, even when lit, on winter evenings, by a bare bulb in the grimy ceiling. There was always that funny smell, too. A mixture of scuffed lino, cooking gas, bicycle grease and cat piss.

Mrs McCarthy, Jer's mother, never smiled; and whenever she spoke she covered her mouth with a hand so as not to show her teeth. 'You break my heart,' she'd shout after Jer when he ran out without asking. And it was true. Though no sacrifice was spared to send him and his brothers to CBC for a start in life, Jer never passed a single exam; most of the time he played truant, filching sweets from the shops, feeding tiny sparrows to his caged magpies, strolling down to the forbidden docks, or – his favourite game of all – lighting bonfires in the quarry beneath Lovers Walk.

Jack and Jer may have been best friends, but that didn't mean there weren't fights. The first fight our gang had was actually about what the gang should be called. Jer suggested the Balubas, but Jack objected – Balubas were the sworn enemies of the whole Irish Army, including Jer's own father! Jer shrugged that one off but made sure to bicker with every suggestion Jack came up with. First, The Boys of Ben Hur. Jer said Charlton Heston was a nobber who hadn't the guts to side with the Romans and finish off the Christian slaves (he and Jack had seen the film in the Pavilion cinema the week before). Besides, Jer said, it was a cog of the local Cork anthem, the Boys of Fair Hill. Jack then suggested a series of names borrowed from pop groups of the time – the Tivoli Trogs; Beaky, Mick and Titch; the Montenotte Seekers; Sam the Sham and the Pharaohs – but Jer ridiculed each one, especially the last which he said sounded like a list of old mummies.

We were in a fix. And things only got worse when Jack started to insist that Maggie – still his crush – should be allowed into the gang. Jer had a fit, and said no gang in Cork had girls in it, girls couldn't keep secrets, they couldn't fight and they couldn't hold out under torture. Besides, said Jer, it was bad enough for Jack to bring me, his brother, into the gang, but if he started bringing in girl cousins as well, we may as well stay at home and call the gang the Cosy Kitchen.

The gang would have split if it wasn't for TV. Just about that time, Father brought home a television set. We stared for hours at the blank, snowy screen, as Father sorted out the wires and signals. Then it came, all at once, a shaking black-and-white image, like one of those hidden figures appearing through a page of invisible drawing – only these figures were moving and speaking. It was *real* magic, lighting bonfires in our souls, and Jack decided there and then to take our gang names from the first film we saw on that screen.

The Man Who Shot Liberty Valance. Everything about it grabbed us. Liberty Valance (Jer), the bad guy terrorizing good guys. Tom Donovan (me), the local ranchman rival of Valance. Ransom Stuttard (Jack), the tall hero played by Jimmy Stewart. And Vera Miles (Maggie), the girl every guy wants to get when the showdown's over.

Names at last. Names of people we could dream about but never be. Bearing these new nicknames we'd ride away from our families into a brilliant sunset. Better than baptism names, or confirmation names, these were names from a bigger world – a place we'd never been, a place where anything might happen.

Only one thing was missing – the name of the gang itself. The Liberty Valance Gang was floated by Jer but immediately shot down by the rest of us. We did agree to his second suggestion, though – Cork Hibernians. They were the local cup team and we were fans, all four of us, even Maggie. Besides, we liked the fact that Cork came before Hibernians.

The gang met on Saturdays and Sundays at the bottom of Corkscrew Hill. Saturdays we'd usually head down to the Palace or Pavilion for one of the half-price matinées. We saw *Mutiny on the Bounty* twice, *The Great Escape* three times, and *Fifty-Five Days in Peking* so often we lost count (it stayed longer in Cork than Charlton Heston stayed in Peking). Sundays we'd take the bus from St. Luke's across the city to Flower Lodge where Cork Hibernians were taking on one of their rivals – Shamrock Rovers, Limerick United, Bohemians, Dundalk Town, Sligo Rovers, Waterford.

No Team's a Match for the Boys of the Lee! That was the Cork Hibs anthem, even though many of the Boys in question weren't from the Lee at all. Some spoke with cockney accents and could scarcely find their way around the city centre. Two such blow-ins from the English Second Divison were Charles Digginton and Bill Wavenport – known locally as 'Diggy' and 'The Wav'. When they first signed, there was an effort to disguise their Englishness by giving them names from New York gangster movies – Fingers Marciano and Babs Capone – but nobody was fooled. Charles Digginton and Bill Wavenport were more cockney than the Artful Dodger. We settled for Diggy and The Wav.

They were the jewels in the Hibs crown, and they were a right pair. Their fame on the Flower Lodge field was equalled only by that off it. Especially down in the Arcadia where they'd do wild versions of the Hucklebuck whenever Brendan Boyer and his band played the venue. Cork gave them more leeway than she gave her own, mind you: they were English, after all, so Protestant; Protestant, so fancy-free. If they made it with Cork girls, more power to them. It was only a venial sin – not a 'more-teller', as Jer would say. Besides, the local girls were mad about them, forming lines in front of the dressing room to shout 'Spit on me, Diggy' or 'Give us The Wav' as the two boys dashed out to play. Diggy and The Wav became lead scorers in the League, memories of Cromwell and the Black and Tans quickly forgotten. More Cork and more Hibernian than Cork Hibernians themselves! Everything was hunky-dory. Until the black striker from Bohemians scored a hat-trick.

It was a bitter day and Cork Hibs and Bohemians were vying for top of the League. Flower Lodge was full of chanting as the teams jogged on to the field, but a hush descended when word shot round that the black centre forward on the opposing team had just been signed from an English side. Bevies of schoolgirls from Miss O's and Scoil Mhuire responded to the challenge with a local number:

> Come on Diggy, Come on Wav
> bring us glory bring us luck
> Come on Diggy, Come on Wav,
> boys who never pass the buck!

But Diggy and Wav had met their match. The stocky black striker was booting shots into our goal-mouth at a fierce rate. There he was, flaking down the wing, side-stepping our goalie and slotting clean strikes to the back of the net. Diggy tried, again and again, to make some mark but the Bohs lad was too much for him. A cry could soon be heard rising up from the back of the crowd – 'Take off Diggy! Bring on The Wav!'

Such fickleness was new for the home supporters, but sure enough, after a matter of minutes, off strolled Diggy and on came The Wav. He fared little better, though; and after several spectacularly unsuccessful slides and sweeps, The Wav too bowed in shame as the Bohemians striker netted his third goal. Three nil. A hat-trick.

> Go home Diggy! Go home Wav!
> Go back home to England!
> Go back home to England!

The crowd roared even louder, as the home team trailed off the pitch for the break. Only our gang, it seemed, stayed true. I looked over to Jack who was staring about him, arms akimbo, disgusted with the carry-on. And it got worse. A small group of gurriers just in front of us launched into a new chant:

> Take the wog off the field!
> Take the wog off the field!
> Send him back to Africa!
> Send him back to Africa!

I turned to Jack and said I thought it was terrible. But Jack didn't hear with all the shouting. Somebody else did, though – one of the gutties right in front of me. He must have been the leader of his gang the way the others stood back to let him through as he turned around to face me, head on. He took two steps forward, until he was right level with me, and said: 'Comeeransahdat!'

But I couldn't 'come here and say that'– he was standing less than an inch away. I could smell his stale cigarette breath and see the hate widening his eyes. My heart was loud inside me. I couldn't say a thing.

'Comeeransahdat!' he hissed again, this time through thinner lips. Once more I struggled for words as a sort of screen came down over my eyes and I saw Ransom Stuttard and Tom Donovan and Liberty Valance and wondered what they would say if they were here. But none of them spoke, none of them whispered words in my ear to save me, no secret messages to help me out. I'd have to fight this one on my own. I stepped back from the guttie, raised a hand to my mouth, and facing around towards the open pitch, roared, 'Take the wog off the field!'

Cork Hibs lost the league. And after a while Jack and Jer decided we'd simply call ourselves 'the gang'.

I never fought the guttie; but I did end up having a fight with Jack soon after. There was no real reason I can recall. It happened one day we were going out through the gate and bumped shoulders. Jack threw me a mock-punch and I went for him. He tried to shrug me off at first, holding me in a neck lock with his strong red-haired arms. He kept laughing every time I bucked, not wanting things to turn nasty. Until I twisted free and stared into his face, saw no hate, and spat between his eyes. He lashed back then, giving me a dead leg, as he wrestled me to the ground. I tried to spring back, arms flailing, cursing Jack over and over. But each time I lunged at him, he swung me down until I finally felt like I was acting out a nameless script, making Jack do this in spite of himself, as if we were both part of some TV story.

Entry 10
Cork, December 1966

I never liked Jer McCarthy. Maybe because he was Jack's best friend. I don't know. When his nickname, Liberty, lapsed, he wanted to be called 'Mac'. It had a hood ring to it, sharp and curt and macho. But I kept calling him Jer, and so did Jack.

He never talked much, Jer, but when he did it was always talk of sex. And it was just that, talk. Any time a good-looking woman passed by he'd do a fake swoon and swear he'd eat chips from her knickers. We'd laugh at that, even Maggie. But as she laughed she'd lift her eyes to heaven, sending a tiny line through her brows – a habit she'd taken from her mother. Jer shrugged off Maggie's put-down; but it got to him somewhere.

Maggie was beyond Jer's reach. Irritated by his con-man swagger and boast to know every song of *Revolver* off by heart, she was always putting him down, driving him to distraction. But the more Maggie scorned Jer the more he fancied her. Jack saw all this, of course. He knew Jer was no rival. He didn't seem to know that I thought I was.

Maggie had a cropped fringe that curled flat against her forehead when she ran, and a slightly turned-up nose with freckles in summer. Sometimes, if she tired of our antics, she'd withdraw into herself and rub her eyeballs with the sides of her wrists until star showers fell inside her head. Her mother taught her that too, and said it was the 'efflorescence of the soul'. With her rough gear of boots and loose pullovers, Jack said Maggie was a cross between Mia Farrow in *Guns at Batasi* and Audrey Hepburn in *Charade*. But I thought she was more like Gia Scala in *The Guns of Navarone*. Jer said he didn't give a damn who she looked like, he'd eat chips out of her knickers anyhow.

'Checkpoint Charlie' changed all that. It was a simple game invented by Jer – spying on a crippled neighbour called Old Ma Daly as she undressed. At first it was only for Jack and himself. But I made such a fuss, I was allowed in after a while. Never Maggie. Jer insisted on that.

Just turned sixty, Old Ma Daly had feather-white hair and thick glasses. She spent her days in a wheelchair because of some accident she'd had long ago, and only left her bedroom to take her evening bath. Fridays at six, we'd meet by a large oak tree overlooking Ma Daly's house in Montenotte Road. The all-clear sign was an up-down tune Jer whistled through his teeth, followed by an owl call blown between clenched hands. Hearing that, we'd scamper up the ladder to the top of the tree – our 'Checkpoint Charlie' look-out – and stare across at Ma Daly's.

Ma Daly had a huge house, four storeys high. One higher than ours, three higher than Jer's. Jer's brothers told him the house once belonged to a lady called Sarah Curran, mistress of the great Republican martyr, Robert Emmet; their affair ended when the British hanged Emmet after some rising in the last century, and the garden lodge where the lovers met was burned in reprisal. It was well after that when the Dalys, wealthy importers of rubber and one of Cork's Merchant Princes, bought the main residence, eventually using the gutted lodge to store tyre remoulds.

We'd sit on that tree, across from the house, staring at squiggles cut deep into the bark – initials, arrowed hearts, unreadable obscenities – as we waited for the game to begin.

Six o'clock, on cue, the bells of the Angelus chimed simultaneously from St Luke's Church below at the cross and the radio inside Ma Daly's room. The low voice of Charles Mitchell groaned through the news as Jer trained his dad's field glasses on the window opposite. He didn't need binoculars, of course – : 'Checkpoint Charlie' was less than ten yards from Ma Daly's bathroom. He sometimes let Jack look too, who said it made him right up close, as if he had her all to himself. Jer never let me look.

For someone in her sixties, bedridden and half blind, Old Ma Daly had, Jer insisted, a 'mighty body'. The show began, after the news, when her handyman, Old Connie Henchy, wheeled her into the bathroom and left her. Alone by her basin and bath, Ma Daly began her ritual undress. Each gesture was precise and poised, like a dancer at the Opera House. First the hairnet slowly removed, hairpin by ivory hairpin. Then the nightdress, raised above her head with elegant arms. And, finally, the layers of underlace, unbuttoned one by one in a downward shedding of veils, slipping away on either side in a pale-white dance of flesh. Folds upon folds uncoiled before us – from breasts to tummy to bottom and thighs – as she moved from wheelchair to bathtub. And, dazed by all that weaving of skin, we stared, half closing our eyes to take it in more fully, as the mauve nipples of her breasts gazed back at us, like adders through thick panes at the zoo, warning us not to come closer.

There was more. Ma Daly's elaborate washing complete, she'd raise herself up by the side rails of the bath and turn towards us to release a glimpse of dark triangle down below. The shock of black against white thighs was like a mouth opening in a wake of surf to suck in air and light. Then the fluent body disappeared again behind a swell of curtains.

Show over, Jer lit a Sweet Afton and would ask Jack, with a Steve McQueen smile, what he thought. Had he a hard-on when he saw Ma Daly's fanny? Had he noticed she had white hair on top but black below? Did he know she had five meals a day and could eat an entire chicken on her own, sucking each bone clean as a whistle? And how come she was called 'Ma', if she never had babies?

Before Jer got his answers, 'Checkpoint Charlie' was busted. Maybe I'd begun to hate the Jer-Jack duo or something, I don't know. Maybe I was fed up with being the odd guy out. Or maybe it was a way of saying to Maggie that I fancied her just as much as Jack and Jer, and even more. I honestly don't know. All I know is I told Maggie of our game, and one day she followed us to the hide-out. Things were in fine swing when she burst in on us. We wheeled around to see her standing there on top of the ladder, a tremor in her face coming and going, as though she were concentrating on something inside her head. '*Peeping Toms!*' she finally screamed at us.

The words dropped from her lips like a bugle-blow. Jack turned away. But Jer was furious. His chin quivered and grew hard. 'Checkpoint Charlie' was no longer a dare-devil act by the Berlin Wall. And it was Maggie – the one Jer wanted more than anyone, the one he couldn't have – who was ruining everything. Jer moved towards her and put his face right up to hers. A shiver passed through his big shoulders, his muscles tightening then loosening in a shrug. 'Fuck off and leave me alone,' he spat into her hazel eyes. The last words he'd speak to Maggie.

Two nights later, fire lit up the Montenotte sky. Jack woke me in the middle of the night. 'Sam, get up,' he said. 'Cork is burning!' Father was already dressed, ready to bring us down the road to see the flames. He seemed as excited as us, and as we hurried towards the blaze, loose gansies over our pyjamas, he told us about the Black and Tans setting fire to Cork when he was a boy. And the Opera House going up in flames in '56! As we got closer, we saw it was the tyre storage in flames – the old lodge Sarah Curran lived in all those years ago, long before the Dalys bought the place.

Half of Montenotte and Mayfield were already there, huddling close, glad to be children again, wide-eyed before the blazing fire in spite of everything – rivalries, fears, class. We were all one before the white heat. 'Something so simple about fire,' somebody said. And I thought of all those Bible stories we'd read about in school – the Burning Bush, Sodom and Gomorrah, Abel's bonfire, Tongues of Pentecost, Hell.

The voices seemed to thicken as newcomers arrived, St Luke's Church booming away in the background. Uncle Dick came over to us with Maggie and Veronica, and we stood close. We stared at the coils of flame hissing and spitting into the air. The black tyres, stored in piles, were furling and unfurling in a belly-dance of death, exulting in the frenzy of some pent-up, long-forbidden power – the moment come, the waiting over. I stood by Jack's side, spellbound by this snake-dance of destruction. Black rubber, red flame, gold smoke. Colours of the CBC blazer. *Christian Boys Hurray! Christian Boys Hurray! Evan-ivan-ee-zoh-zum! We're the Boys who drink no rum! Rum-rum-rummy-rummy-rum-rum-rum-rum*!

Jack nudged me just then and pointed to the McCarthy brothers fanned out in a line opposite. We made signals to Jer but he didn't respond. Jack was upset, I could see, closing his eyes and opening them, as if wanting to give some nod of recognition with his eyelids, as if there were things he wanted to say, grieving things, hard things, things he couldn't say. But the leaping flick and spit of the flames soon recaptured his gaze, and mine, fumes of molten rubber stinging at our throats, the heat punishing if we went too close. *Evan-ivan-ee-zoh-zum!* The chant kept running through my mind. *Evan-ivan-ee-zoh-zum!* It was still running when the cry went up.

The crowd loosened, then jerked to alert. Jack pointed over to the big house. 'That's where the cry's coming from!' he told us. There she was, Old Ma Daly, standing by her bathroom window, surrounded by billowing sails of smoke. It wasn't meant to end like that.

While firemen were attending to the blazing lodge, flames must have crawled across the property, winding their way up our 'Checkpoint Charlie' tree ladder, and darting tongues on to Ma Daly's house. Now, staring towards her bathroom window, splintered by heat and fogged with steam, we knew those cries were hers. By the time the fire brigade got there, there were no more cries; and nothing of the body was recovered from the ashes. It wasn't meant to end like that.

There was an obituary in the *Cork Examiner* some days later. Jack saw it and read it aloud.

Mrs Nelly Daly, née Mulcahy, was born in Cork in 1904. She married Finbar Daly, a Commander in the British Navy in 1922. He was shot several months later by the Black and Tans in a case of mistaken identity. Commander Daly was returning with his wife Nelly from a dinner with a close friend, John Barry, well-known Cork Republican. The Crown forces mistook Daly's car for Barry's and opened fire. Commander Daly was fatally wounded while Mrs Nelly Daly received a bullet in the hip, crippling her for life. The car was chauffeured by Mr Connie Henchy who also suffered injury . . . Mrs Daly lived on for a further forty-four years until her accidental death in the recent fire at her Montenotte home.

Several weeks after the fire, Jer failed his Primary Cert and left for England. He never wrote to Jack or made contact with us during his few visits home over the years. Only Maggie heard from him, once, a tourist postcard of the Berlin Wall.

Thinking of you here at Checkpoint Charlie.
Liberty Valance is alive and well.
Jer.

Jack and Maggie were always convinced that Jer had started the fire. I let them believe it.

The following summer a French girl came to visit us in Myrtleville. Her name was Violaine, Violaine de la Motte; but everyone in Myrtleville knew her as the 'Tolands' French au pair'. The truth is she was never our au pair. She was Maggie's language exchange partner, and both of them stayed with us that summer because Aunt Madeleine was in hospital.

'Here comes the Tolands' French au pair,' locals used to say as she cycled through the village on her way to Poul Gorm. She certainly made a big impression. On me and Jack above all. Violaine was a sixteen-year-old beauty from Narbonne. She had wine-dark skin and brooding sloe-eyes, even darker than her skin; and she used to wear coloured cord sandals called *espadrilles*. The blustery weather made her moody a lot of the time, but she always came to life when she heard music. Her face lit up, and her body became alert, as if flexed to spin. Jack said she was the sexiest thing ever seen at the Myrtleville hops. Especially when she slow-danced to tracks from the *White Album* – 'Julia', 'Happiness Is a Warm Gun', 'Sexy Sadie', 'While My Guitar Gently Weeps', and her favourite, 'I'm So Tired.' She'd actually mime the words with her wide lips as she peered over the shoulder of some swooning suitor: they were the only consecutive sentences of English I ever heard her pronounce during her two-week stay. And she didn't even pronounce them, she mouthed them.

What struck me first about Violaine wasn't her looks, though. Or her English. It was the way she said the word *d'ailleurs*. The curt *d'aill-* followed by the long, rolling back-of-the-mouth *-eurs*. I often tried it when I was alone, moving my tongue from the top of my teeth to the pit of my mouth. But I could never say it as she did. And I didn't know exactly what it meant; though I guessed it had something to do with changing tack, crossing from one thing to another, an extra twist of the tongue, second thoughts.

Sometimes, especially during bad weather, Violaine stayed in her room for hours. When I'd ask her what was wrong, she'd reply: '*Fiche-moi la paix*' or '*Je boude et toi alors!*' Then her eyes would go blank again, as if a veil had been pulled behind them. I thought *boude* had something to do with 'boudoir' (as Aunt Madeleine called her dressing room with a mocking voice). There was something soft and forbidden too about the pouting *ou* sound. As for *fiche*, I supposed it must be to do with water or the sea.

My ignorance of French didn't stop me reciting Violaine's phrases back to her with a Cork accent. This made her giddy with laughter, and sometimes earned me a hug. And even though I was three years younger, she once held me so close I could feel her breasts through her tee-shirt and smell sun-oil on her skin. After that, Violaine left the door to her room open more often. And if she was in one of her moods, she'd teach me bits of French songs and have me repeat them in my funny up-down accent – the opening lines from 'Tous les Garçons' by Françoise Hardy or the chorus of 'Michèle' by the Beatles. I'd sing and Violaine would reply with a song about a sailor boy navigating unknown seas. She'd laugh as she sang, looking out from the black pools of her eyes.

> *Il était un petit navire,*
> *il était un petit navire,*
> *qui n'avait ja-ja-jamais navigué,*
> *qui n'avait ja-ja-jamais navigué,*
> *ohé, ohé, matelot,*
> *matelot navigue sur les flots,*
> *ohé, ohé, matelot,*
> *matelot navigue sur les flots.*

The round O of her mouth – for the last word, *flots* – made my heart roll over every time. I forgave her everything then: the way she sulked with Maggie, the way she turned her nose up at our food and was always asking Mother for exotic cheeses and yoghurts, the way she ignored Jack and me in public, only having eyes for older boys. I even forgave her for almost driving Maggie anorexic, never eating a pick, sucking her cheeks into a moue, and wearing skin-tight jeans to turn the heads of fellows at the Myrtleville dances. But Maggie was all right, I reckoned. She had Jack.

There was no doubt about it – Violaine made quite a name for herself at the Sunday night hops. Within days of her first appearance, stories were rife about her going the whole hog with the tennis champion from Fountainstown, Mugs McIntyre, known to his cronies as The Mighty Quinn because he was endlessly imitating Manfred Mann. He boasted that Violaine had given him a gobblejob behind the hall, and would have gone the whole way if he'd had a johnny. Jack and I knew it was just talk. Mugs McIntyre was even worse-looking than Jer McCarthy. We couldn't help noticing though that Violaine became more desirable the more she was desired. It seemed part of her magic, that desire of desire. Every guy in the village agreed, the 'Tolands' French au pair' was the best thing to come to Myrtleville since Thunderclap Newman's 'Something in the Air'. It was in the air all right: Paris, Prague, Chicago, Myrtleville . . .

I always thought Violaine had a special thing for me. She knew I had a crush on her, of course. And sometimes she seemed to play on it a bit, as if it amused her. One afternoon, for instance, when Jack and I were skimming stones with some guys in Poul Gorm, she walked straight down past us, head bent as if following some invisible tracks in the scalloped sand, and dived into the water. She swam out to the south rock, exposed at low tide, and sat there for several minutes. Catching our eyes, she waved. Jack and I waded out and swam towards her. We breaststroked through the water – freezing even in July – towards the rock; and halfway there, Jack gave me an elbow, nodding towards Violaine, and I swallowed a mouthful of water. Looking up, there she was, posing side-saddle on the seaweed rock, breasts naked, her dark head thrown back towards the sun, as if drinking in some celestial nectar.

Our very own *petite sirène*. A first for Myrtleville where no one ever swam topless except for unseen skinny-dippers late at night. Violaine had imported nude bathing from the beaches of Roussillon to the coves of Cork; and I was sure she had done it, that day, specially for me. Jack had Maggie. Fine. I would have Violaine.

My crush on Violaine wasn't all in my mind. Before she left she taught me how to kiss with tongues. The French kiss, like everything good, happened at the end and took me by surprise. The night before Violaine caught her plane home to France, I brought her a present of a costume jewellery bracelet I'd saved for. She was in her room packing when I gave it to her, and she laughed quietly as she slipped it on, raising her upturned palm in the air. A curious light curved through her eyes, making them brighter, almost opal, She turned to me and whispered, as if part of a conspiracy, '*Merci.*' Then taking the two sides of my face between her hands, she drew me to her.

'*Tu m'aimes bien, alors, mon petit?*'

Yes, I said, also in a whisper, my Adam's apple taking a jump.

'*Tu veux que je t'embrasse avant que je parte?*'

Yes, I said again, not knowing what she was saying, but knowing.

'*Bien, mon petit matelot, attends-moi.*'

Violaine rose from the bed where she was sitting by her open case, walked towards the light and turned it off. She came back towards me then, walking in the dark. Sensing her approach, I turned towards her, waited. Her hand sought out mine and, lifting it slowly, pressed it against the downy nape of her neck until I touched the place her hair curled in a crest. I could see nothing but felt her breathing close to mine. Her sweet breath wove a softness of air about us as her lips came over mine, then between them, coaxing them open. Her tongue touched my teeth, and touched again, in small waves, gently lifting as it moved into my mouth – navigating, *sur les flots*, her tongue turning around my tongue now, criss-crossing, several times. Like a slow-motion dancer offering more than she will give, savouring a bouquet without swallowing, knowing the magic moment of delay, giving the tongue time to move from the *d* at the front of the mouth to the *eurs* at the back. That's why I'd have died for Violaine just then. *D'ailleurs*.

Some days after she'd gone, I fell upon letters lying on Jack's bedside table, signed 'Violaine'. I only read a few lines, enough to realize she'd been carrying on with him throughout her stay. Jack, I shuddered, throat tightening, had been there before me, had crossed tongues with Violaine, maybe lots of times, before that last night, without my knowing. But worse, I suppose, was the feeling that Jack had left the letters there so that I'd read them; and that, yet again I was turning and turning in some cold space, following the lines of an elliptical curve, always drawing ahead as I approached. Trying to catch a fleeting figure by the heel.

I placed the letters back on Jack's table and looked out through the bedroom window. It was an overcast day, nothing unusual, but there was a different slant of light in the clouds just then, as if the sky was melting into rain.

Entry 12
Myrtleville, July 1969

I didn't want to go to boarding school at first. Jack did but I didn't. Perhaps I was taken by a notion of striking off on a different path, doing something on my own, being able to be me for once without being him. Father was irritated by my reluctance and kept going on about Columbanus Abbey being less than a hundred miles from Cork. As it happened, I changed my mind at the last minute and went after all. Though no one ever knew the reason.

It was 20 July, 1969. Jane Fonda's big day. 'Hanoi Jane Strikes Again', ran a caption in the *Cork Examiner*. And there she was, on the middle page, star-turned-commie sitting astride the barrel of a Viet Cong tank. There was lots else in the paper that day. Mary-Jo Kopechne, twenty-seven years old, found dead in Edward Kennedy's half-submerged car in Chappaquiddick. A call for a new inquiry into Rolling Stone Brian Jones's drowning in his Essex swimming pool. An interview with Mid-Ulster MP, Bernadette Devlin, on the riots in Belfast. Ann Jones's defeat by Billy Jean King at Wimbledon. A feature on the recently appointed Bishop of Kerry, Eamon Casey. A report from Cape Kennedy about the imminent moon landing of Apollo II. But the one story that lit bonfires in my mind that day was Hanoi Jane crossing the lines to consort with the enemy.

I cut out her photo and pasted it to the wall. It was the thirteenth shot of Fonda to be added to the collection Jack and I kept in our Myrtleville bedroom. Staring at the line of faces that day, however, I felt like a lost wanderer surveying an unreadable map. Hanoi Jane looked terrific, of course, with her metal helmet and bullet-proof vest. And the voice of Credence Clearwater Revival on the record player was just right. So right there was something wrong.

It was while changing records – *Abbey Road* for *Bad Moon Rising* – that I heard voices from the conservatory below. Mother was talking to someone. Who? Certainly not Father; he was seeing patients in Cork at this time. Nor Jack; he was out fishing for the day. It took me a few moments before I got it. The person conversing with Mother downstairs was Aunt Madeleine.

I listened then for Maggie's voice, and Veronica's; but they weren't there. Aunt Madeleine must have driven down by herself for the afternoon. The older I got (I was now fourteen) the more I began to notice Aunt Madeleine. She was small – smaller than both her daughters, who had shot past her at puberty. But what she missed in height she gained in style. Apart from some disturbance in her soul, Madeleine was all finesse. Her hair, fetched up at the back, was fair, so fair in fact she looked like one of those stunning Icelandic women from the *National Geographic*. Her eyes, under a high forehead, were pensive and deep, flashing with pleasure whenever Mother got her to recall growing up in Glasgow and the many handsome men whose heads she'd turned. A wide smile lit her face then and her sculpted features livened. Aunt Madeleine rarely spoke, it's true, but when she did she'd search in a careful way for just the words she wanted. Her slightly accented voice never rose above a certain pitch, giving her an air of detached, uncluttered attention. And whenever she finished what she had to say she'd often lean her head back a fraction and look off to a point somewhere in the distance. Even when she was there she always had the allure of being elsewhere. That's why I lusted after her. Even more than I'd lusted after Maggie, or Veronica, or Violaine.

Aunt Madeleine was half-Scottish. Born and educated in Glasgow, where her parents went to live after her father qualified in law at Queens, she was sent to finishing school in Fribourg in Switzerland. That's where she met Mother and they became best friends (she disliked the other girls, she said, with their privileged pouts and prissy ways). It was Mother who invited her to spend the following summer in Kinsale and introduced her to Uncle Dick.

Aunt Madeleine liked to wear white dresses, often with a purple scarf. Mother said she wasn't only her best friend but the best-looking woman in Cork. Jack and I agreed. We compared fantasies with each other once and came out evens. Only Fonda came near Aunt Madeleine. Unlike Hanoi Jane, though, our aunt disliked politics with a passion. Except when it came to mocking the latest royal escapade recounted in the *Illustrated London News*.

That day I listened to every word Aunt Madeleine spoke. I'd overheard her mention my name to Mother downstairs and went out on the landing to hear better.

'It's such a shame Sam won't go.' Aunt Madeleine was speaking, her tone unhurried, almost docile. 'It would make him more of a man, like Jack.'

'Why don't you tell him that some time?' said Mother.

'I'm not his mother.'

'But he has a soft spot for you, Madeleine, you know that.'

'So you always say. But what about Jack?' Aunt Madeleine paused. 'Surely *he* can get round Sam?'

'He's tried. Sam won't hear a word . . .'

'I thought they were inseparable – the Toland Twins and all that?'

'They were, Madeleine. They always were, even though Sam's heart kept him back at first. But it seems to have changed this last year. Before, Sam wouldn't do anything different from Jack – now he won't do anything the same. I don't know.'

'Well, I'm afraid I can't help, Angela.'

'He'd listen to you, though, I'm sure of it. Remember

those letters he sent you last month, the ones Dick opened by mistake . . .'

'That's just puppy love. Adolescent fantasy. It has nothing to do with leaving home to go to boarding school, I can assure you!' Madeleine paused a moment, then continued. 'Though I admit it takes some puppy to copy out Valmont's letter to Madame Tourvel from *Les Liaisons Dangereuses* and plant it under my pillow.'

Mother offered Aunt Madeleine a cup of tea, but she said she'd try something a little stronger. There was a brief shuffling of feet and glasses, before Aunt Madeleine spoke again. 'I don't know, Angela. If I were to be entirely honest, I'd have to admit I find the whole thing a bit pathetic . . .'

'Why?' Mother sounded wounded.

'Why? Because you've molly-coddled Sam all these years – ever since he came out of hospital with his baby chest sewn up – and then you wonder why he won't grow up . . .'

'But he needed special care . . .'

'Children thank you most, in the end, for the things you *don't* do for them. You'll see.'

'I don't see. And I don't like what I think you're getting at. More of that Freud business you're always on about. Devouring mothers and little boys competing to be fathers. Mine aren't like that . . .'

'Maybe they're not little boys any more, Angela. Maybe they're changing. You really should read the letters Sam sent . . .'

'I don't want to see them. That's your business. Mine is knowing that my boys don't think the way Freud thinks they think . . .'

'All Freud said, Angela, was that no child is innocent.'

'Well that's just it. I *do* believe children are innocent. And I believe that line in the Gospel too about it being better to be cast into the sea with a stone around your neck than to corrupt an innocent . . .'

Madeleine interposed, 'We're not talking about corruption. We're talking about sex.'

'Yes, all right, but it's not like that for children, that's all I'm saying.'

A little exasperated now, Madeleine responded, 'You remind me sometimes of those Swiss nuns, Angela, always going on about sex being something the angels didn't need because they were so close to God.'

'Maybe they had a point!' Mother said. 'And maybe your problem, Madeleine, is that you only see the black side of things.' Pause. 'If you could actually *believe* in something, anything, some basic goodness in the world, in God.'

There was another silence. I imagined Aunt Madeleine putting her hand to the spiral curl clasped behind her head, as she always did, her mouth lifting in a smile.

'I'd just like to see you happy, Madeleine, that's all. And I'd like to see our children happy too, for as long as they can be.'

'I know that's what you mean.' Madeleine spoke gently, then more boldly. 'I know that's what you want. But life isn't like that, Angela. It doesn't begin happy and it doesn't end happy. Women aren't Virgin Marys – and men aren't Saint Josephs. Children find that out quick enough, no matter how long you keep them from the edges. The more protected they are, the harder it is, the more it hurts. If they're addicted to perfection, they'll take a terrible knock, I tell you. Because this world is full of inexplicable things, unspeakable things: sex is one of them. And despite what all the holy books say, sex is what makes us tick. It's what makes us love and hate; it's what makes us lie and betray and save and create. It's never black or white. Freud got it right, Angela, we're not angels. We've all taken a bite of the apple. Sam and Jack too.'

'We're not going to agree about this, I know,' Mother said. 'But let's not argue. Tell me about Maggie and Veronica . . .'

'My, my, I must fly, dear Angela.' I imagined Aunt Madeleine lifting her shoulders in a concluding way and rising from her chair. 'You've reminded me I've to collect the girls in town on the way home. I'm already late!'

That's when Mother called to me to come and say goodbye to Aunt Madeleine. As I came down the stairs, Aunt Madeleine raised an almost-empty glass, jiggled it, and put it down on the table again. She stood there, as I approached, the evening sun growing thinner as it drained out of the room through the bay window. Her eyes were lambent, cornflower blue. I hadn't noticed before. Better than Hanoi Jane any day, I thought, as I kissed her on the cheeks, twice, hello-goodbye. She laughed as she got up and moved towards the door. We saw her to her car. When she'd gone I told Mother I had something to tell her. I'd go to Columbanus Abbey with Jack in September.

The next day, 21 July, Neil Armstrong stepped on to the moon. But my mind was full of other things.

*

So that's what decided him!' Jack says to himself out loud, slapping his hand down on the page. Summer heat, Thunderclap Newman, fantasies of a Hollywood vamp turned communist, and a stray remark from the lips of a sexy aunt. That's all it took to change the direction of Sam's life. The perfect reason to leave home for a monastery.

Jack considers the absurdity of it all, staring at the row of Priscian files lining the shelf in front of him. But he is troubled. There are things emerging in Sam's story which are deeply baffling to him. He is surprised to learn that Sam had lusted after Violaine that way. Jack had left the letters by his bed to make Sam jealous all right. But he never knew that Sam had got so close to Violaine and fancied he could win her. Sam had been following Jack like a shade all those years, he now realized, coveting his desires, trying to have what he had, to be like him, to be him.

Jack is uneasy now. He closes the journal, and looks across at the icon of St Gallen hanging from the wall above Sam's bed. He notices a small inscription on the parchment carried by the angel: 'God calleth the things that are not as though they were' (Romans 4.17). Then he looks up towards the angel's face, staring deeper and deeper into the eyes until he imagines Sam staring back at him. Angry? Mournful? Playful? Coy? The signals are confused. What would Sam tell him now were he there? What would he say about their rival adolescent lustings after Maggie, Madeleine Violaine? Their fascination with Jer McCarthy? Their last images of Ma Daly? Yes, what would Sam say about that now? Would he really insist he was the one who started the fire? Or admit it was just another version of the way things might have happened, the way things had to be for Sam to become what he eventually became? Ma Daly, like Mary Murphy – another terrible oblation on the altar of Sam's calling and salvation?

Jack wants to know. But would Sam ever have agreed to tell him what was real and what imagined? And why it mattered? The Angel of St Gallen is mute. Its small lips sealed. Its eyes blank. Wings impassively folded behind shoulders and halo.

'It does matter,' Jack murmurs to himself. 'It matters to me.' His long arms hang down by his sides, motionless for several minutes. Then he turns back from the icon to the journal on the desk, opening it again where he'd left off.

THE LIFE OF TOBIAS

PART THREE

'Let each examine himself – since the son should not
be degenerate and the disciple should not contradict
the master in his preaching; for he that does not
enter by the door into the fold of the sheep is a thief
and a robber . . . May I be allowed with your peace
and charity to enjoy the silence of these woods.'

The Works of St Columbanus, Epistula II, 3–6. AD 603

S

Mother saw us off at Cork station. She couldn't look Jack or me in the eyes. Jack tried to cheer her up saying she was worse than Scarlett O'Hara losing her beloved offspring in *Gone with the Wind*, but it didn't work. A wounded stare came and went in Mother's eyes, a stare of not-knowing. She tried to put on a brave face when Brother Cilian introduced himself on the platform and took charge of us. I could see Mother sizing him up – this tall Cistercian novice with a good-humoured face and high cheekbones – and deciding her sons were in good hands. Though this didn't stop her turning her head and weeping helplessly when she tried to wave goodbye.

The train rattled away from the platform and entered a black tunnel. Brother Cilian went to get us mugs of tea at the bar. Jack looked out of his side of the window and I, sitting opposite, looked out of mine. I put my forehead to the window and thought about Mother. I felt for her when she cried like that. And now, leaving her, I realized she'd always been doing it, ever since I could remember. Almost anything could get her going. The death of one of Father's patients, the sight of a shawlie begging with

babies on Patrick's Bridge, a horse being put down at a
Mallow point-to-point, a matinée weepie in the Pavilion,
a sad scene from the Coachford Pantomime at Christmas.
What really got her going, though, was leaving for holidays
each May and having to leave Jack and me behind. Father
would smile and take her by the shoulder, teasing her with
the old dance refrain:

> Jeepers, creepers, where d'you get those weepers?
> Jeepers, creepers, where d'you get those eyes?

When Cilian returned with the drinks, we asked him to tell
us about Columbanus Abbey. Up close he had smoky breath
and nicotine-stained fingers (he always had a cigarette
between them). Laughter lit up his face every time he
spoke, or sneezed, which was often. He talked non-stop,
in fact, filling us in on countless things as we tossed our way
north towards Roscrea station. He himself had entered the
Order at the age of eighteen, having been a student at the
Abbey where he was fortunate enough to have discovered
his calling under the tutelage of Abbot Anselm.

Anselm, he explained, was the youngest abbot in the
country, elected at the age of only thirty-six on his return
to Ireland after years of study on the Continent. He had
particularly distinguished himself as a linguist and exegete
at the renowned monastery of St Gallen in Switzerland. It
was there he took his name from the eleventh-century saint
who devised the famous proof of divine existence from the
Idea of Perfection. Everyone at Columbanus Abbey was
devoted to him, monks and pupils alike. Even the mothers
of the boys were mad about him – he was that handsome.
Cilian's broad face broke into a smile before composing
itself again. Anselm was someone 'alive in Spirit', a holy
'leader of men', a real 'doctor of souls', an exceptionally
'pious monk'. Cilian emphasized each phrase as if reciting

incantations from a litany, commonly shared formulae which – true enough – Jack and I would come to make our own in time.

Cilian paused, briefly considering. For a second he seemed to be measuring his thoughts against the rapidly passing landscape, synchronizing his words to the rolling rhythm of the carriage. Then, touching a stained finger to his forehead, he resumed his little speech. Columbanus Abbey was called after the eponymous Irish saint from the seventh century, and was not to be confused with the Columban Order founded by a different Irish saint, Columcille. The Abbey was run by the Cistercian Order, celebrated for their 'mystical piety'. Cilian stopped at this portentous phrase to take a drag on his cigarette, as if preventing himself from saying too much. But in that momentary lapse, I had already gleaned a hint of things to come.

The first abbot of the monastery, Cilian continued in a matter-of-fact tone, was a certain Father Tobias, a Swiss monk sent over from St Gallen to Ireland at the turn of the last century to take charge of the new Abbey. Although Columbanus Abbey looked old, it wasn't really old at all. In fact, it wasn't even an abbey originally but a Big House built by Protestant gentry, the Rawn family, in the late eighteenth century. It was designed in quasi-medieval style – grey limestone, turrets, slit windows, fake drawbridge – and was flanked by colossal oaks and forests of assorted rare trees imported into the country by one of the Rawn brothers, an amateur botanist serving with the British Legion in the colonies. It was the same Colonel Douglas Rawn who had built an artificial pond named the Black Lake to the south of the house, deceptively shallow owing to surface weed. The estate actually found its way into Cistercian hands less than a hundred years ago, when one of the Rawn sons was shot during the Land League Campaign and the family decided to move, selling the property for a

modest price to the local bishop. It was he who offered it
to the Cistercians, explained Cilian, to establish a school for
sons of wealthy Catholics. Several ministers of the State had
been educated there, even a former Taoiseach who qualified
with first place in maths in the national exams.

We were met at Roscrea junction by the headmaster,
Dom Basil, a small barrel-chested priest with widely spaced
eyes, hair twisted back, and little purple stains on the flesh
of his nose. He welcomed us in measured tones, virtually
ignoring Cilian, and said we'd have to wait half an hour for
the train from Dublin to arrive on the opposite platform. I
didn't like him. On the twelve-mile bus ride to the Abbey,
I sat beside Jack and watched the boys who joined us from
Dublin as they cavorted with confident gestures and noisy
hoots. I didn't like them either.

When we arrived, Dom Basil divided us into two groups
and showed us to the new-boys' quarters. Jack and I were
in different dormitories. Most of the boys in mine seemed
to know each other, having attended the same prep school
near Dublin – St Jerome's – before coming here. They stood
around, faces coarsened with acne and faint hair growth,
their arms folded as if they'd been in the place for years.
When they spoke they all sounded the same, and hearing
I was from Cork they did imitations of my up-down accent.
The 'West Brit Brigade', I christened them, knowing what
Terence MacSwiney must have felt like when he first ran
into the Black and Tans. I looked up at the kindly face of
the icon on the wall and kept to myself, unpacking my wash
things into my bedside locker and concealing my transistor
radio under my pillow. (I was still a fan of Radio Caroline).
Outside the dorm windows, the sun was going down behind
a confusion of clouds, and the air had that uncertain light
of coming rain. It was only an hour to Vespers; then I'd
see Jack.

When Vespers rang, I followed my dorm-mates down

the long corridor towards the church but lost them on the way. As I approached the Senior Dorm, a crowd of prefects was gathered at the door. 'New scut! New scut! Dirty little new scut!' they jeered as I passed. Fear was making my heart thud against my ribs when I suddenly glimpsed Jack emerging from the stairs behind me. 'New scut! New scut! Dirty little new scut!' the shout continued. I saw Jack stand there for a moment, as if caught in a freeze-frame between clips, taunting Seniors on one side, me on the other. There was panic in his eyes, a flicker of uncertainty. He didn't say he was my brother. He behaved as though he didn't know me. That's all the Seniors wanted. They let us pass.

Next morning we had exams. Dom Basil arrived with papers and pencils and explained how the class would split into two streams depending on results. I knew Jack would make the A class (he was always first at Christians) but feared I'd end up in the lower grade with the Jerome's boys. Irish was the first test, and I strolled through thanks to CBC which had made me fluent in the national language. Then history, geography, English. Fine. Finally maths; I was always useless at maths and Jack was on the far side of the classroom. That's when I put my hands over my face, sucking in air, and bent forward on to the desk in tears. There was commotion in the class as Dom Basil escorted me into the corridor to background sniggers from the West Brit Brigade, sure of triumph now.

Basil brought me to the infirmary in the west wing where the nurse, Miss Bernadette Birch, diagnosed my condition as nerves. She looked just like Irene Papas out of *Zorba the Greek* with her black-brown eyes and dark skin. 'You'll settle down soon,' she said, putting her cool palm to my forehead, confining me to bed for the rest of the afternoon. And lying between the sheets of the infirmary bunk I thought, if pen is mightier than sword, as Terence MacSwiney said, tears are mightier still.

That evening I arrived in Assembly to find the new boys gathered round the notice board. Results were out and, as I neared, I heard one of the Jerome's boys complain in a high-pitched voice, 'Those Cork twins made it into A grade, both of them!' Jack and I were still together.

Entry 14
Columbanus Abbey, September 1969

'Why have you come here? Why are you here? I will tell you. You are here not solely to pass your Leaving Certificate, not solely to please your parents, not solely to put a label of distinction on your blazer front. You are here to learn something more, something else, something about another kind of journey. *Itinerarium mentis*. What Columbanus called the journey of the soul towards Perfection. If this Abbey empowers you – as I pray it will – it will be with a power of listening, a power of discernment that will set you free. That is my hope for each of you.'

Abbot Anselm spoke his first words to us, the new boys gathered together with the rest of the school, in the high-ceilinged assembly hall looking out over the rhododendron gardens flanking the Abbey. The Inaugural Address was delivered each year in the same place at the same time – before six o'clock supper on the first Monday of term. The Abbot's voice was unhurried, as if rehearsing a script aloud to no one in particular. There was something intangible about his words, and about him, a sort of total self-containment, maybe selflessness.

Looking up at Anselm from the front row where I sat with Jack and the new boys, I noticed how his hands were a little too large. How his face was white, emaciated, almost lipless when he spoke, but strong-jawed, with chiselled forehead and features. And his eyes? Difficult to tell at first, as he rarely looked at us when speaking but stared into some middle space beyond the window at the back of the hall. When he did look down, however, they were unmistakable – pools of pale blue light. Bottomless, impersonal, near-transparent, as though incapable of subterfuge. Like the eyes of the icon that hung upon the wall behind his head, the Angel of St Gallen. They made me shiver, whether with fear or love I could not tell.

Abbot Anselm went on that day to speak about the famous Rule of Columbanus, eponymous spirit of this Cistercian abbey. He told us of the age-old quest for a perfect liturgy which might reveal the ways of God to man and reunite the fragmented Word of Christ – a quest that had inspired so much of Western monasticism from the outset. Columbanus and Gallus, twin patrons of the Abbey, were exemplary symbols of this quest, the Abbot reminded us. Trained in the monastery of Bangor at the end of the sixth century, they sought to unite two apparently conflicting sides of spiritual life – contemplation and action – and made their motto from the simple formula 'Blessed is the soul wounded by love, for in its wounding it is always healed . . . Let him be emptied and filled with God who wishes that his prayers may all come true.' With this message the two saints embarked on a migration through pagan Europe, accompanied by eleven disciples, founding missionary settlements in such far-flung places as Luxeuil, Annegray, Fontaines, Bregenz and, of course, St Gallen, to this day our kindred abbey. The Rule of Columbanus guiding these monasteries took the form of a Path of Counsel for an elect of chosen souls whose vocation was the Way of Perfection, and whose means was a threefold practice of Discretion, Mortification and Contemplation of scripture. Chastening themselves through rites of confession, under the tutelage of a director, Columbanus's disciples became

'soul fellows' (*anamcharaid* in Irish). The common aim
of their penitential was to disclose God's hidden Word,
unifying the split tongues of Babel and repairing the rents
in the garment of the spirit.

But the most lasting teaching of Columbanus, Anselm
emphasized with an almost ethereal pitch of voice, was
the mystery of *possession through dispossession*. A mystery
exemplified in his famous prayer: 'May our loving quest
for Thee, O Lord, occupy our every inmost thought; that
thy love may take complete possession of our being and
so fashion our senses that we may know not how to love
anything else but Thee.' Only this hunger for a divine Word
beyond us could hope to reunite our disseminated selves, a
hope recalled by Columbanus to Pope Boniface in a letter
deploring schisms – 'make us members of one Body of Christ
. . . the Logos of God!'

These Columban precepts, Anselm proclaimed with a
concluding gesture, would soon become part of our lives as
pupils of this school. But our task would be a more modest
one. Unlike Columbanus and Gallus, whose travels brought
them through the by-ways of the Continent, our journey
would be an inner one, a journey through the testing
waters of the Spirit. Anselm's face glowed, as determinedly
inscrutable in that moment of initial epiphany as it would
ever remain.

After his Address, the Abbot dismissed the assembly with
a large hand, inviting the new boys to accompany him
on a tour of the grounds. Jack and I followed behind
the Jerome's boys as Anselm led us through the church,
with its ochre ceilings and white walls, its dark side aisles,
high pillars and classic Roman archway. He pointed in
passing to the closed wooden door of the out-of-bounds
Icon Chamber. This, he informed us, housed the precious
St Gallen collection, on loan from the sister abbey in
Switzerland. Then he ushered us down towards the Black

Lake, past the rhododendrons, Spanish chestnuts and Scots pines (he named each type of tree in turn), out along the back avenue lined with African cypresses, Douglas firs and Giant Redwoods (his favourites) across the gateway into the old forest of Ilchester oaks. And as he strode before us, the Abbot rehearsed the wonderful lines from Hosea: 'I will be like the dew to Israel. He shall strike root like the forests of Lebanon. He shall again live beneath my shadow. He shall flourish as a garden . . . O Ephraim, what have I to do with idols?' He fell silent then for a good while, pacing away with deliberate, rhythmical steps at the head of the group.

On the way back, Anselm had us recite aloud after him the Latin names of each tree – *sequoia sempervirens, sequoiadendron giganteum, rhododendron arboreum, pinus montezumae, quercus petraea.* We jumbled these unpronounceable sounds in our mouths and laughed. And maybe that was the beginning of Jack's love of trees. I don't know. But I do know that the words of the Abbot's first address, uttered in unhurried tones, radiant and level as his pale eyes, remained with me for years, becoming more and more engraved on my mind each time he pronounced them, every First Term of every year, in the same assembly hall, to the entire school, before he took the new boys off to visit the grounds, the church, the gardens and the lake.

Entry 15
Columbanus Abbey, 1969–1971

We revered Abbot Anselm. But it was Brother Cilian, still only a novice, who was our best teacher. Jack's and mine. Officially assigned to teach Latin, he mostly taught us other things. Extracurricular things like philosophy and philology which he'd studied in Paris, along with his theology at the

Saulchoir. Whenever he became excited about his subject in class, which was often, Cilian would sneeze one of his inimitable sneezes: it would gather up inside him like a breeze, until he'd have to stop, mid-sentence, eyes narrowing to slits, mouth sucking in air, as the squall came gusting from the pit of his lungs through flaring nostrils. The entire class would hear it coming, like an air-raid siren, and take cover under lifted desktops – only coming up to glimpse the blanched hue of passing turbulence flee from Cilian's face as he resumed his teaching undisturbed. Even the Jerome's boys had to admit Brother Cilian was 'great gas'.

In our first Latin class, Cilian arrived with a copy of *The Aeneid*. Without introduction, he just began reading – as if continuing an on-going conversation with himself – a passage about Dido falling for Aeneas:

> *At regina gravi iamdudum saucia cura*
> *vulnus alit venis et caeco carpitur igni.*

Then he paused, and added another line, learned by heart it seemed – *Ac nunquam, aestivo conspectus tempore glaucus.* Not knowing one word of Latin, all those sounds rolled over our heads – *saucia cura, carpitur igni, tempore glaucus* – reminding me of the stray passing voices picked up on foreign radio stations. *Prague, Ankara, Lahti, Stockh'm, Lisbon, Geneva.* Magical vowels and consonants, incomprehensible diphthongs, and lots of incantating verbs, verbs, verbs. But this was different from the radio. And different from the sound of Latin at Mass or plain chant at Vespers. Here was a monk possessed by script, by the story of man and woman, a story of so-called 'secular' love. *Saecularis, Saeculum,* Cilian explained, a world of time, of circles, a world that takes time, a world of difference. Like Dido feeling the flame of love return to her breast when she beheld Aeneas, and knowing no matter what she did it was going to happen all over again. *Agnosco veteris vestigia flammae . . . et tacitum vivit sub pectore vulnus*. 'I recognize the signs of an old passion. The wound still bleeds silently in the heart'. I didn't know how Cilian knew so much about wounds of the heart, but he did.

On that day, as on many another, Cilian read whole passages, again and again, without pausing. He knew we'd respond to the music of the words, if not to the words themselves; and that we'd want to know more, to feel ourselves what Cilian felt as he relived the passions of Dido and Aeneas, entering their foreign world, climbing each rung of its ladder until we reached the secret of that faraway tongue.

'What I want to teach you isn't Latin,' Cilian would say, 'it's to imagine words as things.' Each word, he'd then explain to us, is a trace that makes distant things near, foreign things familiar, absent things present. Not literally present, of course, but magically present, *as if* they were here. Aeneas and Dido standing before us in the classroom! Carthage come to Columbanus Abbey! That was the secret of language, Cilian said, imagination as a two-way ladder with opposite words going up and down, meeting halfway, crossing over, interweaving, translating, displacing. Binary opposites, yes, exchange of contraries. Dialectic of the gemini. Fall of Carthage, rise of Rome. Fall of Dido, rise of Aeneas. Fall of Remus, rise of Romulus. Fall of Gallus, rise of Columbanus. Each sign betrayed, each sign restored. Each sign restored, each sign betrayed. Learning a language, Cilian concluded holding back a sneeze, wasn't just apprenticeship to *meanings*. It was more than that, much more – it was an endless hunt for things that didn't exist, an interminable play of signs, each displacing the other in an infinite game of desire. Language was *desire*, not fulfilment of desire. That's what he'd learned in Paris and that's what he believed.

Cilian had learned other things in Paris too. Like a love of drama – his 'first mistress'. Sartre was his favourite playwright and he'd seen most of his plays performed in Le Vieux Columbier in the early sixties with François Périer and Madeleine Renaud as leads. He'd even gone to listen to Sartre and Simone de Beauvoir speak, standing on biscuit boxes, to workers outside the Renault factory in Paris, and nursed a secret dream to invite them both to Columbanus Abbey one day when he returned to Ireland. Well, the dream didn't remain secret long. Getting carried away during a class one morning, he wrote a letter to them explaining that even though Columbanus Abbey was a Catholic monastery devoted to the education of Ireland's bourgeoisie, it would be a great honour to have them speak to us – on, say, anxiety and the proletariat as conditions of freedom!

Not knowing their address, and drawing a blank with their publishers, Cilian sent off the letter anyway, addressed to *Monsieur Jean-Paul Sartre et Madame Simone de Beauvoir, c/o La Préfecture de Police, Paris*. It got there.

We heard nothing for several months, but when we did – a registered telegram from Paris – there was ecstasy. Cilian waved it in the air with his nicotined fingers, and read aloud:

Mon Cher Père.
Merci de votre invitation. Non, Simone de Beauvoir et moi ne voudrions pas rendre visite à votre Abbaye de bonne foi. Nous avons d'autres choses à foutre que de papoter avec des jeunes privilégiés sûrement destinés à devenir la prochaine génération de capitalistes sans conscience!
Salutations,
Jean-Paul Sartre et Simone de Beauvoir

Cilian jumped in the air and sneezed. Hadn't the great

French existentialists written to him 'personally'? And what
if they couldn't accept the invitation? Hadn't they written a
perfectly heartfelt statement of their anti-bourgeois convic-
tions, and signed it – that was the best of all – *Salutations!*
The free-thinkers of Saint Germain assuredly had no idea
what pleasure their letter of abuse gave their Irish Catholic
recipient.

I suppose that's what Jack and I loved most about Cilian
– the way he often got things wrong. Especially words. Like
when he misquoted Macbeth to Jack before a Munster final,
telling him to 'stick his courage to his screwing place and
he'd not fail'; or when he urged one of the cleaning ladies,
who'd been stealing from the dorms, to 'make a clean
card of it and put her breasts on the table'; or when he
sent a Cistercian dissident in Prague my end-of-term Latin
report and my parents a letter encouraging them to resist
harassment by the secret police!

Cilian was a terror for mistaken messages. Slips of the
tongue, malapropisms, spoonerisms, you name it, he was
a past master. He was for ever getting names wrong too –
calling me Jack and Jack Sam for as long as he knew us.
Maybe that's why he was always so obsessed with language
– and especially accounts of its origin. Given half a chance,
he'd sound off on theories about the Perfect Tongue, some
of which he'd learnt from Anselm as part of his novitiate
research. He'd rehearse the genealogy with great panache,
making fulsome, sometimes mock-heroic gestures with his
outstretched hands. As if he were on stage.

First there was the undivided Logos existing before the
Fall, the pristine alphabet Yahweh used to create the world
and Adam used to name the animals. Then Babel and the
division of language into many tongues, scattered over the
nations of the earth; and the story of the *Sefer Yetzirah* or
Book of Creation, containing secret letters of Genesis which
God first gave to Abraham and Shem so they might learn

its inscriptions and recreate another world; and the advent of Christianity calling the divine Son *Verbum* or Word, and revealing how he wrote letters in the sand and taught in signs and left a Paraclete after him who spoke in tongues; and how the great Doctors of the Church spent centuries trying to recover the lost language of Creation, but never succeeded, even in the Latin Liturgy of Holy Rome, because after Babel there was no going back. Crossing tongues was the original sin of language, Cilian told us. And the best we mortals could do now was use our imagination, (or *yetzer*, as the Hebrews called it) to retrieve odd connections between different tongues, making words play so we might feel what others felt and understand our foes a little better. That was the best we could do – make words play. To do more than that, to presume we could find the meaning *behind* the words, that was impossible: the reason Adam fell, Babel fell, and Gallus fell.

It wasn't obvious how much of this Cilian was taking from Anselm, and how much was his own. But I could never help suspecting there was some inner struggle being played out. Especially when it came to Gallus.

Yes, Gallus! Cilian would set off on his own tack, his broad figure pacing the schoolroom energetically. Disciple and fellow-traveller of Columbanus! Founder of Europe's most inspiring monastery in the seventh century, and subsequent scriptorium of medieval renown! St Gallen, our sister abbey of prayer and learning where our own Abbot Anselm had completed his studies in Scripture and prepared for ordination! Gallus, Brother Gallus, who became so taken by the search for the celestial Word he forgot his feet were on the ground and tripped on thorns and lost his eyes! A lesson there somewhere, Cilian concluded with a theatrical spread of his hands, his smoky eyes dancing almost in spite of themselves.

Cilian performed this ritual litany on several occasions,

always with that singular mix of piety and exaggeration that was his hallmark. One day, however, the ritual was followed by a big debate. Jack asked Cilian if there could ever be a perfect language again, with each word meaning *one* thing. Cilian said he didn't think so as every human language had different meanings for words and different words for things. Cow in English was *vache* in French, *Kuh* in German, *bó* in Irish. Names were matters of custom, invented and reinvented by various peoples in various places, things we create, signs we exchange, like women exchanged between tribes as Lévi-Strauss had shown. A question of symbols not substance!

Did that mean we could also name things that *didn't* exist, Jack asked, as intrigued now by the puzzle as Cilian himself. In a way, yes, it did, admitted Cilian, citing the famous example of medieval philosophy – *nulla rosa est*. Here, he explained, we have words naming the *non-existence* of something – the rose that *doesn't* exist – *as if* it existed. The rose that *is not* becomes present to our minds thanks to words. Absence becomes presence. But not 'real presence', he added, scrummaging in his pocket for an invisible cigarette. Not real presence, no. Pretend presence. Imaginary presence. Playful presence.

By now Cilian was in full flight. Forgetting he was still in class he almost lit up a cigarette, and ran off a rapid list of further examples – from the mystic's 'rose without why' to the poet's 'rose of nobody' to Stein's 'rose is a rose . . .' But the real fun came when he got to Romeo's line 'What's in a name? A rose by any other name would smell as sweet.' Would it? Jack asked. Would Juliet seem just as sweet if she were called, well, 'ass-hole'? The Jerome's boys sniggered into their desks at this, especially Geoffrey Nash and Donal Harrington, who were always glad to see Jack go too far. Jack was pushing it all right; but Cilian was in ecstasies, beyond scruples about propriety. Jack continued his barrage of questions. How could Juliet's *being* remain as sweet if her *name* changed? Wasn't *Romeo and Juliet* a play, after all, about how names – Capulets, Montagues, whatever – make us what we are whether we like it or not? And aren't we all like that, carriers of names we never chose, names given to us at birth, names we can't change without changing our selves, or hiding behind pseudonyms, taking on fake names? Isn't that, after all, why so many people get upset if you mistake their name – because they feel you're mistaking their identity, getting them wrong somehow?

Cilian laughed out loud at this delicious river of queries. It was milk and honey to his soul. His broad face became broader, his high cheekbones higher, his short breath shorter, the more it went on. He was delighted with Jack and – calling him Sam by mistake as usual – said he was as quick as St Cyril who started asking questions from the time he could first speak and ended up inventing the Slav alphabet! Along with his brother Methodius.

That's how Jack and I changed nicknames for a time: from Castor and Bollox to Squirrel and Method. The Jerome's boys would call after us in the corridor, especially Geoffrey Nash with his loud-mouthed sneer, but we didn't care. Jack took it in his stride, like another fumbled tackle on the rugby field. And I was even chuffed, secretly pleased that words might soon be mine, the secret power of language no longer secret, withheld, deferred. Cilian's magic, I vowed, would soon become mine, mine to call my own. Someday I'd find the answers to Jack's questions.

Entry 16
Columbanus Abbey, 1972

Drama was Cilian's 'first mistress'. Jack and I often had to compete for parts in the end-of-term plays he directed. Jack, being taller, usually got the lead. I found myself playing Mephisto to his Faust, Andreas to his Galileo, Horatio to his Hamlet, and (hardest to take) Seaneen Keogh to his Christy Mahon. Though I wasn't an original, Cilian always consoled me with the fact that I was a gifted mimic. It was true. I could take off almost anyone, gestures, features, bearings. And I could pick up accents in a flash. I had a good ear. I was a good listener.

When it came to film, Cilian's 'second mistress', however, I found my place in the sun. Despite a strong challenge from Donal Harrington, I was elected auditor of the school's Film Society, set up by Cilian in fifth class. We saw several New Wave films that first season, recommended by Cilian from his time in Paris – Resnais, Bresson, Fellini, Truffaut, Visconti, Godard. We even got to see some of the first American colour classics in the second term. Elia Kazan's *East of Eden*, Jack's favourite, with the shot of Adam kissing his girlfriend in the barn full of melting ice cubes as the jealous brother Cal (James Dean) looks on; and Hitchcock's *Vertigo*, my favourite, where the retired cop Ferguson (Jimmy Stewart) is hired by his best friend to spy on his mystery wife (Kim Novak). I was puzzled by the fact that Ferguson had two names, Johnny and Scottie. And the mystery wife had three – Madeleine, Judy and Carlotta. I saw it several times while we had it on hire, relishing and reliving each scene. The opening frames of Ferguson's nightmare – head spiralling down through empty air off a steep roof. The bit where Carlotta Valdes leaps into San Francisco Bay only to be saved by Scottie who takes her home and changes her black and white clothes for a scarlet polka-dot gown. (Kim Novak looked the image of Aunt Madeleine in that scene.) The shots where Scottie takes Carlotta to a clothes shop and makes her dress up like the 'real' Carlotta. And the last sequence where he drives her to the old Spanish Mission to discover who she is, dragging her through the whitewashed cloisters with her grey-green dress and dyed blonde hair pinned back in a spiral curl, up the winding wooden steps and out on to the balcony where the crime is re-enacted all over again – and the victim falls to her death.

Having seen it several times, I knew most of the lines by heart, reciting them out loud to Jack and the others in a fake American drawl. I got the Jimmy Stewart almost perfect (better than Jack ever did doing Ransom Stuttard), though my Kim Novak was always a little hoarse. But I suppose what struck me most of all was the fact that Scottie Ferguson was fascinated by the same trees as Abbot Anselm, the Giant Coast Redwoods – *Sequoia sempervirens*.

Cilian's own favourite film was *L'Âge d'Or*. And it proved in a curious way to be his fall from grace. *L'Âge d'Or* was one of Buñuel's earliest black-and-whites, with English subtitles. We'd ordered it for the gala mid-term showing and sat, boys and monks alike, in the big hall, wide-eyed before those flickering grainy images: bishops chanting blessings for invading armies, a monstrance exiting from a taxi, maids running screaming from a blazing kitchen, a gardener shooting his own son dead, tumbrils driven through crowded salons, and the final sequence of Christ himself emerging like a criminal from an all-night orgy.

Dom Basil protested vigorously after the showing. The film, he insisted, was an assault on the Catholic Church. He remonstrated openly with Cilian for permitting such material to be shown to impressionable boys. Cilian might have said nothing, and that would have been that; but he replied, upping the ante, claiming education was first and foremost about seeing the other's point of view, and that if Christianity couldn't understand Buñuel's atheism it could understand nothing! Basil was enraged and, next day, circulated a three-page stenographed paper to all pupils as we filed into the refectory. Entitled 'Pornography, Art and Religion', it berated Buñuel as a cynical corrupter of morals. By the end of the following meal, Cilian was back on the attack, surrounded by a halo of cigarette smoke, distributing a Reply, 'Still an Atheist, Thank God – A Note on Luis Buñuel', in which he argued that Buñuel's surrealist film was an attack not on religion itself but on the temptation to make the Church into a second Tower of Babel, the idol of a second *âge d'or*.

The battle split our class into rival camps. I supported Cilian, as did Jack and most of the others. But some of Basil's camp, orchestrated by Harrington and Nash, resorted to dirty tricks, circulating all parents with a letter complaining of the liberties Cilian was taking with the Film Society. This got to Cilian. A terrible heaviness came over him when he first heard of it, a sort of tightening inside.

Not wishing to drag Abbot Anselm into the mêlée, and lacking support from confrères (Basil was headmaster after all), Cilian sought out a pupil. That pupil was me. When I entered his room, I remember, he was seated, rocking gently back and forth as though listening to music, looking blankly at a woodcut of St Gallen on his wall, then staring out of the window at the Lebanese cedars flickering in the blustery wind. And when he turned at last, in measured degrees, to speak, I could see he'd lost something, some inner light or self-possession. There was a disconsolate look about him now as he fumbled on his desk for cigarettes. Like Scottie Ferguson after he let Carlotta fall from the Mission tower.

'How are the boys taking it?' he asked.

'Fine,' I said. 'Most are with you.'

'Are many parents responding to the circular?'

'Not that I know. But I'd say they'd write to you directly if they write at all.'

'I suppose you're right, Sam. I don't seem to be thinking straight these days, do I? But you've done me proud, keeping the other boys on our side like that. I appreciate it.'

There was something slack about his face as he spoke, his head muscles drawn down as if responding to a pull within his soul. Only his feet moved, jittering away beneath his desk.

'It wasn't hard, Cilian,' I said. 'You know we think you're great. We hate Basil.'

'Well, you shouldn't . . . but I suppose I understand.' Cilian paused, desperately trying to rally himself, to lift his spirits. 'Basil *is* a horse's ass!'

I laughed out loud at that, and Cilian loosened, cognisant of having broken some kind of code, crossed some invisible boundary. And that's when he let rip, talking and talking as if he'd never stop, confiding in me things about his past, little things and big things, personal things, grieving things, hard things; and especially the thing that happened when he was studying in Paris. In his second year of Theology, he met a woman working in the film section of the Saulchoir library; she was older than him, in her late twenties, originally from the Midi. Her name was Pascale Questiaux, she looked like Monica Vitti, and he adored her. She was making money for her studies, translating subtitles for foreign films, and knew every cinema in Paris. They'd often go to showings in the afternoon, and, very soon, they knew they were in love and wanted to live together. He'd leave the seminary, they agreed, and they'd both move in together to a small flat in the rue des Quatre Vents near Odéon. But the day they were to move, he changed his mind. He never met her again, not even to tell her his decision, to say he was sorry, to say it had all been good but it was over now. He just pushed a letter under her door and took a plane back to Dublin.

Cilian fretted as he spoke. There was a cloudiness about his eyes, as if bits of his past were breaking free from the sea-bed of his mind and floating up to the surface. A milky whitish film seemed to be forming in his irises; and tiny red veins curled at the edges of his eyes. He looked away when he'd finished speaking and, shaking sediment in a whiskey glass, stared through the window at the thick light trawling the tops of the cedars. Then he checked himself, thanked me for listening and apologized for telling me, a pupil, his 'secrecy of guilt'. It wasn't really right, he said; he hoped I didn't mind.

I felt a rush of elation. It was me Cilian confessed to in his moment of need! I was the chosen confidant, sitting alone like Jacob with Isaac, listening to his words, savouring his voice. I was the one receiving his blessing, his preferment, offered like that in total trust in the shade of the afternoon. Closing the door behind me, I glided down the corridor and headed for the gym. There I found Jack, as I assumed I would, and told him what Cilian had told me. But Jack was confused, I could see, pushing his hair back nervously, looking away. I realised, in a flush of panic, that I shouldn't be repeating things like that, even to Jack. And especially not in a gym where anyone might hear. What would happen if Nash or Harrington or the Brit Brigade got wind of it? Could I keep nothing to myself?

Next day Cilian called me to his room again. He was calmer this time, more withdrawn. He told me he'd just had a call from Basil saying that his Paris story was doing the rounds of the Abbey. There was no real option, Basil advised, but to leave graciously before it became an issue. Cilian raised his upturned palm, sensing my panic, and told me he didn't hold it against me, that he knew it wasn't me who talked to Basil, it was somebody else; it didn't matter.

At the end of that term, Cilian left Columbanus Abbey for his annual summer holiday and didn't come back. He wrote to me once, though, shortly after he left. The envelope smelled of cigarette smoke when I opened it and I could imagine him with his blurred eyes and broad open face, a Gauloise between his lips. He couldn't finish his novitiate, he wrote, despite the Abbot's efforts to persuade him. He could no longer carry the burden of the calling, the weight of expectation, the role prepared for him as Anselm's chosen protégé, sent to study in Paris so he might return and assist him in his quest for the lost Tongue. Anselm had guided him all the way, from the beginning, enthusing him with his research on sacred grammars, making him feel unique, elected, irreplaceable. He felt Anselm's terrible grief at his leaving, of course; but he knew now he just didn't have what was required – the inner discipline, the calm of spirit, obedience to the Word. How could he follow in Anselm's footsteps, become a 'missionary of the secret Logos', when he couldn't even keep his own secrets? How could he observe St Columbanus's first Rule of Discretion, he added humorously, when he was always letting his own tongue slip? Betraying things that should never be spoken? More was demanded of *real* monks. Patient attention to a higher Voice. And a choice between desire and God. He no longer believed in that choice, he said. For people like him, it was a ruinous dichotomy. His vocation had been a mistake. And if he regretted anything, it was leaving Pascale Questiaux behind in Paris. Some people were made to reach God by embracing this world, he concluded, others by surrendering it. He was of the first kind, he'd discovered. And so, he thought, was I.

He added a postscript with a Latin tag, *Dilige, et quod vis fac.* Love, and do as you will.

Entry 17
Columbanus Abbey, April 1973

In sixth class, Anselm began to take a special interest in Jack. Commending his achievements on the field (where he was chosen for Munster's schoolboy rugby team) and off it (where he continued to excel in his studies), the Abbot encouraged him to undertake a special botany project on the flora of the Abbey for the Young Scientist competition. He invited Jack for field tutorials on the successive plantations of the estate, from the enclosure of the oak forest by Royal Patent in 1683 to the implantation of Giant Conifers by Douglas Rawn in the eighteenth century. I'd sometimes encounter the two of them strolling through the grounds, the Abbot pointing to some rare species of cedar or pine, his large hand outstretched and pale eyes steady. My chest would tighten then and I'd feel, for a blind moment, a rush of complicity with Harrington and Nash.

I didn't realize it at first but Anselm's growing interest in Jack did not seem motivated by secular concerns. Only gradually did it dawn on me, as I watched Jack observing Anselm presiding at the daily liturgy. He looked with rapt attention at every ceremonial move the Abbot made about the altar, relishing each sacerdotal gesture, scrupulously imbibing each homily and benediction. He even took to rising early for six o'clock matins and spending hours in the Abbey library reading old scriptural texts which Anselm had on loan from the St Gallen collection. Witnessing this show of devotion and learning throughout several weeks, there was no longer any doubt in my mind: Jack was being groomed for a vocation. And it wasn't long before the other seniors were whispering amongst themselves. Who would have believed it? Jack Toland for the cloister! Next in the succession stakes! Cilian's replacement in the Abbot's heart of hearts!

I was somewhat surprised initially, I must confess, as Jack had always said he'd be an eye doctor like Father. But my surprise was short-lived. The charmed circle was soon shattered. Before the year was out, Jack was summarily expelled from the Abbey. He was asked to leave by Dom Basil in the middle of the last term when found having sex with one of the kitchen staff.

Rachel was her name, Rachel Hegarty, though most of the boys called her 'carrot-tits'. She had red hair like Jack's, but brighter, almost rusty, a hint of soft down on her upper lip, and bare white arms when she served at table with her sleeves rolled up. Lots of boys lusted after her and Donal Harrington boasted he'd have it off with her at least once before he left the school. He never did.

Jack and Rachel used to pass notes to each other with secret rendez-vous while she was clearing the refectory after meals. Mostly they'd meet at the Black Lake late at night and go swimming together in the dark. But sometimes, I knew, they went farther, to the sports pavilion by the playing fields or the circle of cedars beyond the east gardens. I was aware, as time went on, that Jack was beginning to take huge liberties, becoming more casual in his communications, more daring in his games of hide and seek, less vigilant. And the curious thing was that this increase in indiscretion was happening at the same time as his deepening piety. As if he were caught up in some manic flight of fancy, soaring beyond the rest of us as he broke the norms of schoolboy behaviour, his adventures with the illicit somehow concurrent with his newfound agility of spirit.

I should have warned Jack, I suppose, but something stopped me. I could see his dual course was bound for collision. I knew something had to give. But I couldn't bring myself to intercede, or interfere. Like watching someone fall and being fixed to the spot. Waiting for the inevitable crash with frightful, shameful, almost voyeuristic attention. It had to happen. And it did. One evening, after supper, Dom Basil discovered a note from Jack to Rachel neatly folded beneath a plate after everyone had left the refectory. As though in a trance, I followed Basil down the avenue, first to the Black Lake, then past it to the rugby pitches to the east. Basil stopped by the first cluster of Lebanese cedars, listening intently for a few seconds, before bursting through the undergrowth and surprising the lovers locked together, Jack's reddish-brown arms grasping Rachel's white body as they coupled fiercely against the broad bark of a tree. There was uproar. Basil called them two tinkers with their foxy hair and foul carry-on; and Jack shouted back that Basil was a frustrated old celibate with nothing better to do than spy on those who weren't. Jack was asked to pack his bags immediately and not return. The case was open and closed. There was nothing Anselm could do.

It didn't make much academic difference, as it happened, as the Leaving Certificate was only months away and Jack qualified with ease for First Botany at University College Cork. But it did make another kind of difference, a deeper, unspoken difference. Something about a path abandoned, a call unanswered, a plan mislaid. Abbot Anselm tried to appear unconcerned, in keeping with abbatial protocol which prevented him interfering in strictly school affairs. He didn't actually appear for several days owing to what Basil referred to as a temporary illness. But I knew his illness was one deep within his soul.

As for myself, I don't really know what I felt at the time. More a non-feeling perhaps. An absence of feeling. Vacancy. Pure space.

Entry 18
Columbanus Abbey, 11 June 1973

Three months later, after final exams, it was my turn to leave. But I never left. Something changed, changed everything. It was 11 June, the Feast of St Barnabas.

Examinations always made me nervy and I hadn't been eating or sleeping properly during that week of final papers. I was smoking and drinking a lot too since Jack left, sneaking down to the village with Nash or Harrington for a few stiff ones after each test. The neat gins struck home on an empty stomach and I'd end up cranky and sullen, the giddiness of my companions grating on my nerves.

After the last drinking session, at the end of the week, I took refuge in the Abbey church. I needed to get away and chapel after Vespers was the place I was least likely to meet anyone. My head was dizzy from chain-smoking and too many shorts; I was tired from the long walk back from the village. When I held my hands out, they shook slightly. It was there, sitting at the back of the church several hours after Vespers was over, that Anselm found me. He placed the palms of his hands on my two shoulders and gave me the keys to the Icon Chamber. 'Go down,' he said, 'and pray. That is the place you need to be right now.' His voice was gentle, neutral, knowing.

Anselm left and I lifted my head. I looked around. The evening light had already drained from the stained-glass windows and it was difficult to see. The scarlet bulbs of the confessionals had been extinguished, and the only light, a small, thin flicker, came from the sanctuary lamp in front of the tabernacle. The Icon Chamber was behind the altar. Every boy knew that, even though entry was restricted to members of the Order. It was always kept locked and housed a collection of icons on permanent loan from St Gallen.

I say the Icon Chamber was behind the altar but in fact it was *beneath* it. The only access was a small wooden door at the side of the sanctuary, with steps leading down to an underground space. It had been converted from a stone cellar discovered in the foundations when the new church was built. No one was sure if it belonged to the original castle design or dated back to some ancient settlement. One old monk from Kerry, Dom Cornelius the sacristan, swore it was a remnant of pagan worship and that he'd once seen traces of sheila-na-gigs – Gaelic goddesses with naked genitals – on the inner walls before they were covered over when the estate passed into clerical hands. No one believed him; and that's where the sacred icons were stored to protect them from changing temperatures. But if old Cornelius was right, I often thought to myself, what did all those resplendent virgins, saviours and angels feel like beside obscene goddesses with spreading legs?

I opened the door leading down to the chamber. The light was even dimmer down there. One night-candle flickered weakly from a wall. By the bottom step I'd become sufficiently used to it to see my way about. Anyone here? I asked aloud, scanning each corner. I could have sworn I heard someone in the chamber. A faint voice whispering behind my back, from some invisible nook of the room. Anyone here? I called again. Nothing.

It was cool down in the chamber, the dark calming. After a few seconds, the golden frames began to flutter and blur as my eyes grew more accustomed to the half-light. Between the frames faces began to form. Faces of madonnas with crowns and mantles. Faces of messiahs with hands raised in blessing or holding scripts with Greek letters inscribed in amber and ivory. But most of all, faces of angels, white-robed and black-robed, fair-haired and dark-haired, wide-eyed and shut-eyed.

As my eyes tracked back and forth between those angel icons, one face in particular shone more brilliantly than the others. It had a silver halo, red curls and eyes with shining pupils looking straight at me. Smiley eyes.

The more I stared, the more the face appeared to shift and skew, now young, now old, now sad, now laughing, now male, now female. I recognized Maggie and Veronica, Jer McCarthy and Jack, Ma Daly and Madeleine, Violaine and Mary Murphy, Cilian and Anselm. I recognized them all by turn, a funny wildness clutching me, as folded wings rose behind the angel's halo and unfurled in the thin blue light. All the faces were in that face. Even faces I'd not seen before, that took me by surprise, looking out at me from the far side of the icon, the angel's side.

'Why don't you say something?' I thought I heard a voice say, more distinct this time. My heart thumped against my chest as I scoured the chamber.

'There's no one here.' Now I knew where the voice was coming from – the icon right in front of me. It was the angel speaking.

'Who are you?' I asked.

'Can't you read the inscription? I'm the Angel of the Annunciation, St Gallen, seventeenth-century, painted by migrant monks trained at the Zagorsk school after the manner of the great master, Andrei Rublev. You must recognize me. There are copies of me on almost every wall of this Abbey. I'm the original!'

'The Angel of St Gallen?'

'Yes.'

'Are you man or woman?'

'Neither male nor female He created us – as the Bible says.'

'I don't understand.'

'It's like this: we can take on either sex depending on whom we are sent to. When I appeared to Mary and asked her to be with child I was more of a man. But when I appeared to Abraham under the yew tree and broke bread I was more of a woman. And when I wrestled with Jacob through that fateful night in Penuel – the place called "face of god" – I was man and woman by turns. It was the man in me left Jacob wounded and limping; it was the woman who kissed him and told him the name of Israel.'

'So you can change your appearance . . .?'

'Have you not read your Book of Tobit – the passage where I visit Tobias and announce I'm *pure appearance*?'

'No.'

'Well, you must know the passage from Genesis 28 where I go up and down the ladder in Jacob's dream, taking different shapes as it pleases the Lord?'

'Of course. So you're only a dream, then, an illusion . . .'

'Was it illusion taught Tobias to cure his father's sight? Was it mere fantasy that revealed to Jacob the name of Israel?'

'I must go back and read those parts . . .'

'You Catholics seem to learn nothing in your Christian Doctrine classes – except how to avoid the "feeling of angels"! At least Protestants know their Scripture. But then, they're not perfect either: they won't accept *icons* of us!'

'But are you real? Answer me.'

'There isn't an answer for everything, Sam. But I can tell you this much. I am as real as the invisible essence of things, as the fathomless voice where *deep calls upon deep in a roar of waters*. Psalm 44 will tell you all about it. And the Psalms will tell you other things too if you learn how to listen. How nothing is real until voice and vision come together. Words and images. Bodies and souls. Sybils and saints. Mixing. Crossing over and back, up and down, like Jacob's ladder. That's why we angels come at night, in dreams and apparitions, when dogmatists are fast asleep.'

'Why do you come?'

'To remind certain people of a calling.'

'And what is *my* calling?'

'You have the rest of your life to find out. Do keep in touch though, and let me know if you discover something.'

'How do I call you?'

'Any way you like. I have many names. Gabriel, Michael, Raphael, Nathaniel, Jacob's adversary, Tobias's guide, Abraham's guest, Magdalene's ghost, Bethesda's healer, Elizah's visitor by the broom tree. Voices come from me, names from you. I call, you answer. I whisper, you write.'

'But tell me one last thing – who are you?'

'It's not for me to say. The first Rule of Columbanus, remember: discretion. Besides, it's late now. Get some sleep and I'll watch over you for a while. And by the way, tell no one of this meeting.'

'No one?'

'No one.'

'Not even Jack?'

'No one.'

'Not even Anselm?'

'No one.'

Two weeks later, on 24 June, the Feast of John the Baptist, I became a novice of the Cistercian Order.

*

It could have been me, Jack says to himself. If I'd stayed on to the end, like Sam, the icon might have spoken those things to me. But it's crazy. Jack checks himself. Angels talking! Sam must have been beside himself that night. Or maybe it was just Sam's way of convincing himself that he was really chosen, that his vocation was his, that he wasn't simply occupying a vacant space – Jack's space, Cilian's space.

Jack continues to stare at the page in front of him, but he is no longer reading, no longer attending to the words. He is deep inside himself somewhere, light-headed. After a while, he smiles, engrossed in memories. He recalls his first encounters with Cilian and Anselm. How, from the beginning, he'd felt singled out, preferred. Cilian, it was true, had always given him the leading roles. Faust, torn between Gretchen and demons. Galileo, recanting but unbowed. Hamlet, thinking too precisely on the event. Christy Mahon, made real by the power of a lie. Yes, Jack remembers each of these parts, as line after line, scene after scene, comes swimming back into his mind like scattered fish returning to their hatching grounds, feeding off fragments of half-memory. And he remembers too, even more sharply, the special lines taught to him by Anselm – the words of a privileged mission welcoming him to the Abbey; Columbanus's prayers of 'soul fellows', anamacharaid, perfected in 'One Body'; the legendary narratives of Gallus and Columbanus journeying across Europe discovering unknown inner continents each step of the way – Luxeuil, Annegray, Fontaines, Bregenz, St Gallen; the opening words of Columbanus's Rule still echoing inside him: 'May our loving quest for Thee, O Lord, occupy our every inmost thought; that Thy love may take complete possession of our being and fashion our senses that we may know not how to love anything else but Thee.' And the trees. Of course, the trees. The Abbot's Latin litany so often recited on their walks through the Abbey's forests – sequoia sempervirens, sequoiadendron giganteum, quercus petraea, pinus montezumae. Not one of these has Jack forgotten. And that, he's always believed, was why Anselm recited them: so he'd never forget.

But such thoughts do not, in fact, bring him peace. Jack stands up from the desk, surprised by how agitated he feels. He finds himself staring at the woodcut of the old Precinct of St Gallen hanging on the wall above Sam's bed and is baffled by its maze of walls. Adorned by bugled puttis *carrying a titular scroll, MONASTERIUM PRINCIPALE SANCTI GALLI 820 AD, the etching comprises a copy of the Carolingian parchment plan with its outer ring of round towers, guest house, cemetery and school, circling inner rings of cloister, novitiate, scriptorium, library, and, finally, the innermost sanctum of double-choir church and abbot's quarter. A labyrinth of lines, like pasts peeling further and further back.*

It strikes Jack, all of a sudden, that Sam has always been taking his place. And he is even more stunned by the realization of how long it has taken him to register this. Things are beginning to fit together now, though the picture emerging brings no solace. Just as Sam stole his images of the horse and the whale when a child, he had later stolen his privileged space with Cilian and Anselm. He had taken over from Jack, answering the call Anselm had been preparing Jack to answer on those long walks through the oak woods and endless conversations about Columbanus's mission and Gall Priscian and the quest for the lost Logos. But Sam, not he, was the one who found himself in the Icon Chamber to hear the voice of the angel, the one who purloined Jack's part in the Abbot's plan, who ultimately became the novice for the Kingdom of Heaven's sake.

Looking back on it now, Jack sees how Sam had watched his every move, coveting the special attentions he'd always received, picking up the codes at second hand, becoming all the while a shadow initiate without Jack ever suspecting. Borrowing, miming, deriving, plagiarizing. Sam must have sensed he'd finally occupy Jack's space if he was patient long enough, waiting until Jack stumbled somewhere on the path, leaving the way free. Which is what happened. The voice eventually spoke to Sam in the void left by Jack. Sam was the one who entered the Abbey.

For a moment Jack feels something he has never felt before. He knows what it is but recoils from naming it. He knows now with a certainty he's never had before: it is exactly what Sam must have felt during all those years of shading, following, stealing,

*standing in. The feeling of being displaced, of wanting what the
other had. For the first time, Jack is compelled to look this furtive,
skulking creature in the eyes and recognize it as his own, to call
it by its name – jealousy. Anselm was right. Reading Sam's life
would bring him closer to his dead brother. Too close.*

*Jack paces the narrow room, once, twice, glancing in the basin
mirror as he passes. His face is screwed into an unusual shape,
the skin drawn tightly over his cheekbones, anaemic. He is in two
minds. He wants to leave Sam's cell now and wake Raphaëlle and
tell her what is tearing at his soul. But he also wants to sleep, to
blank everything out for a while. He lies down on Sam's bed and
shuts his eyes. But no sleep comes. Instead, the Icon of St Gallen
keeps returning to his mind, speaking to him, just as it had spoken
to Sam. 'The dream of the ladder . . . The struggle . . . Jacob's
double . . . Tobias's guide . . . Neither male nor female he created
them . . . Pure appearances . . . No one . . . Tell no one.'*

*Jack can feel his heart thumping as he lies face down on the
blanket. He knows now he will not sleep, not before he has finished
the journal. Something warns him not to read the final bit, but the
urge to get to the end is overpowering, compulsive. He has to find
out what happens, what becomes of one who listens to the voice.
Sam's story has become a lure Jack can't resist, like a nest of secret
gardens, circling each other in receding rings, trees behind trees,
walls behind walls, each more sequestered, more unsuspected,
more enticing, the further one enters. He raises himself from the
bed and returns to Sam's desk.*

Entry 19
Columbanus Abbey, 21 July 1973

Approximately one month later, Anselm invited me for a
walk. We descended by the Black Lake, crossing Brother
Aidan and Brother Ferdia on our way, and headed towards

the oak wood at the lower end of the avenue. As we walked Anselm recited his favourite refrain from Hosea about 'roots spreading out like the forests of Lebanon' and identified each tree we passed by name just as he always did on the inaugural walk. But this was different. This time, on this day, he was rehearsing the names for me, Brother Tobias. Himalayan rhododendrons, chrysanthemums, tree lupins and azalea ringing the lake. Further down the avenue, past the lake, Spanish chestnut, Scots pine, European larch and Cherry laurel – with a sprinkling of hornbeam and sycamore. Lining either side of the back avenue, clusters of Lebanese and Indian cedars with their stratified, pendulous branches. And as we drew closer to the back gate, giant conifers brought back to Ireland from North America in the eighteenth century by Douglas Rawn. Anselm took a connoisseur's relish in each specimen of this imported plantation. Western red cedars, Douglas firs, Sitka spruces, Montezuma pines; and, jewel of this prized collection, the Giant Sierra Redwoods – *sequoiadendron giganteum*.

We left the back avenue and crossed the road into the old wood, a remnant of the great oak forest that once covered Ireland. Suddenly Anselm began to speak.

'You know the *Gall Priscian*?' he asked.

'Cilian mentioned it once or twice, as I recall, and maybe Jack . . .'

But before I had finished my sentence, Anselm was already explaining. 'It's one of the earliest versions of Priscian's Grammar, located in the St Gallen library. I want you to complete research on a new edition. It will be your special novitiate assignment.' Anselm spoke with animation, giving each sentence a particular inflection.

'Why the *Gall Priscian*?' I asked.

'It has something no other edition has.' Anselm paused, gazing up at the oaks in a moment of uncustomary emotion. 'A curious Index, missing for centuries, which turned up in St Gallen's manuscript archives some months ago.'

'What is in it?'

'That's the puzzle. Nobody knows. It appears to be just a jumble of sentences, randomly selected from the marginalia. But I'm convinced it's more than that. It must mean *something*.'

Striding on deliberately, Anselm spoke to me then, with a zeal I'd never seen in him before. He told me of his own novitiate studies in St Gallen. How he'd travelled all the way to the Swiss abbey to pursue research on the collection of sacred Irish scripts, known as the *Scottici Scripti*. He was persuaded these ancient texts would reveal something of early Christendom's search for a Universal Tongue. It was there he first encountered the *Gall Priscian*. He learned how the Ten Books of this Grammar were first transcribed by Irish monks in the ninth century before being transported to St Gallen; and how the Latin of the main text was annotated in marginalia written in the scribes' own native tongue, thereby recording the first traces of early Irish. The meaning of these coded marginalia, Anselm explained, had remained an enigma down through the centuries. Textual discretion of the subtlest kind. Until, that is, the recent discovery of the index which, he was persuaded, contained some hint of their significance. But the *Priscian* was not St Gallen's only blueprint for a Perfect Logos. There was also the Carolingian Plan for a Perfect Library, the Map for a Perfect Astronomy, and the Scale for a Perfect Music (ranging from polyphony to the Notker scale). Anselm's recurring passion, then and now, was, he confided, to find out if the original Irish monks envisaged their *Priscian* project as a way of retrieving the Language of God before the Fall – the prelapsarian Voice known as *Gairthigern* in Gaelic, *Phonē Semantikē Theou* in Greek, *Vox Domini* in the Latin of the Psalter.

'And what did you discover?' I asked with a rush of fervour.

'I discovered the inexhaustible lust of the absolute,' replied Anselm. He broke off then for a moment, collecting himself before continuing. 'I dreamed of one day getting to the bottom of it all. A dream I have never abandoned. But I cannot complete the work on my own. It takes two, as Scripture tells us, to study God's alphabet. That's why Yahweh insisted Abraham work with Noah, and Ben Sira with his son, in reading the Book of Creation, the *Sefer Yetsirah*. It's one of the oldest counsels in Scripture.' Anselm looked away for a moment, his face wistful, before turning back again. 'I had hoped Cilian would help me with this work. Then Jack. But it was not God's will. You, Tobias, are my last hope.'

'I'll do whatever I can,' I volunteered, my spirit soaring at the bliss of election.

'I'll teach you what you need to know,' Anselm assured me, shifting to a more commonsense tone. 'The basics in calligraphy and script. But you must be aware, Tobias – this is much more than an academic exercise. It is a spiritual task of discernment and discretion, a journey of the soul into secret sacred things.'

'What things?'

'Forgotten traces of a pristine, perfect speech. It will become clear in time . . .'

He lapsed into silence. It was dark in the oak woods now. We had been walking for over two hours. My right foot hurt, the back of my new sandal eating into the skinned heel. I told Anselm and he said we should go back.

As we retraced our path in the dumb light of evening, Anselm began to name the trees again in the same level tone as before, as if our conversation had not taken place. But I wasn't listening. My mind was racing ahead of itself, feasting off images of the *Gall Priscian*, laid open at the centre as it reclined behind a glass casement in St Gallen's scriptorium, its brilliantly illuminated parchment scrupulously guarding the secret of the lost tongue.

Entry 20
Columbanus Abbey, July 1973–July 1974

The 'spiritual exercise' Anselm alluded to on our walk became clearer over that first year of my novitiate. I was instructed to prepare a detailed document on the origins of the *Gall Priscian* and, at the same time, begin a journal recording my inner life – my personal life of memory and desire, my spiritual life of retreat and reflection. This was the twofold practice of the Order's Rule, Anselm explained: study of ancient tradition and study of one's innermost self – the age-old *conversio ad se*. I started both in late September, completing the first three sections of this journal by May. The research on the *Priscian* has been slower. Anselm provided me with a file of relevant articles and commentaries but I still have the impression I'm scratching the surface. Every chance I get, it's true, I arrange meetings with Anselm, usually in the evenings after Vespers, where I ply him with new queries and sit bemused at the marvellous intricacies of his responses. Sometimes we've even talked past midnight, as if possessed by that insatiable lust to know, to find the pattern, splice the scattered hints and guesses into a single thread.

So far, after ten months of research, I've come up with six main hypotheses: i) that the use of old Irish in the disparate marginalia of the *Priscian* is related to the belief, recorded in the Book of Invasions, that Gaelic was composed by Fenius Farsaid and his grandson, Gael Glas, selecting the best aspects of the seventy-two languages of Babel; ii) that the *Gall Priscian* was originally the work of a single author, Máel-Patricc, and not of multiple authors as certain other signatures in the manuscript (Coirpre, Cobthach, Ferdomnach) suggest; iii) that Máel-Patricc was trained as a scribe at the schools of Bangor and Castledermot, thus becoming acquainted with the Rule of Columbanus; iv) that the first vernacular script used by the Irish monks was a purely indigenous hand and not an eclectic mix of borrowed calligraphies – Coptic, Italian, Spanish, Arabian – as some commentators hold; v) that the transportation of the Irish edition of the *Priscian* to St Gallen is to be understood as a direct pursuance of the quest for the universal Logos initiated by the original mission of Columbanus and Gallus to the heart of pagan Europe; vi) that the marginalia of the *Gall Priscian*, listed in the newly discovered Index, comprise a covert formula for the Lost Tongue and are not farcical jottings by Hisperic grammarians opposed to the quest for a Perfect Script.

Anselm declined to confirm my conjectures one way or another. But I knew he was gratified by my diligent persistence. Every so often his lean face would break into a smile despite himself. If anyone could help him crack this code it was me, and he knew it.

As I was working on this material, I had a recurring dream. I kept finding myself alone in a room surrounded by piles of books, each with exactly the same title: *Discretion*. I am trying to read; but I cannot make out the words on the page in front of me; I pretend to read, but I am only making it up; then the letters on the page blur completely as a woman enters the room. She lifts her hair to reveal a bare white neck. I approach her and kiss the warm skin of her shoulder.

I told Anselm the dream. He made no comment, apart from suggesting that I enter it here in my journal. My first novitiate break comes in a few weeks. I need some sea air. Anselm recommends I spend it in Myrtleville.

THE LIFE OF TOBIAS

PART FOUR

'We are all joint members of one body, whether Franks or Britons or Irish or whatever our race be. Thus let all our races rejoice in the comprehension of faith and the apprehension of the Son of God, and let us all hasten to approach to perfect manhood . . .'

The Works of St Columbanus, Epistula II, 9. AD 603

∫

'Where's Jack?' I asked, arriving at the chalet earlier than expected, not anticipating that anyone else would be there.

'Gone for a swim,' she replied, brushing her hair back from her face. Trace of a foreign accent. She was slender, wide-mouthed. She smelled of jasmine.

'You must be Sam,' she said, her caramel-green eyes focusing to a slight squint. 'I'm Raphaëlle. Raphaëlle Feher. I'm from Geneva.' We shook hands.

The sun scattered gold coins on the water and in the side garden, fuchsia and honeysuckle rustled in the sea breeze. The sky was hard blue.

We entered the sitting room together; I left my bag by the bay window, and sipped iced water as Raphaëlle told me how she and Jack had met in Cork. She was a photographer, on assignment for a Swiss magazine. Jack had invited her down for the summer. She loved it here and was thinking of staying on. I hardly listened at first, absorbed by the aqueous light pouring on to her olive-skinned shoulders as she stood by the window.

I was surprised that Jack hadn't written to me about her. But then Jack had kept most things to himself since he left the Abbey. Still, I was curious now and asked Raphaëlle more about herself. She was born in Switzerland to émigré Jewish parents, who had fled there from Prague during the war. Her father died when she was young and she was brought up by her mother, who made a living teaching art history. She herself had studied art and design at Geneva University before becoming a freelance photographer, a job which had taken her on a number of foreign assignments, the latest being this one to Ireland, where she'd fallen in love.

When Jack returned from his swim he behaved as if we'd all known each other for years. He said the water was great and insisted on accompanying me down to Poul Gorm for a dip. Before we went, Raphaëlle took a photo of us standing together with our towels and swimming trunks. 'Les deux frères!' she laughed. There was no sun when we reached the cove, but we dived in anyway. The water was dark, freezing.

I didn't have much further contact with Raphaëlle for most of that week. I suppose I made a point of keeping my distance, spending much of my time alone in the conservatory, catching up on some reading for the new *Priscian* edition, in particular a recent article 'On the Origins of the Old Irish Terms *Goidelc* and *Gairtigern*' and a lengthy piece, 'Sources for the Life of Gallus', just published in *Studia Celtica*. Jack spent his time swimming, pruning saplings in the front garden and collecting specimens of escallonia and hypericum for his botany project at Cork University. Raphaëlle went off for long walks along the shore with her camera. She seemed to enjoy being on her own. There was something self-composed about her, almost self-absorbed. She clearly loved Jack, but didn't really need him. I couldn't quite figure her out in fact. Maybe it was just because she was a foreigner, with her own ways. We all met up for meals, of course, but I always found myself avoiding Raphaëlle's eyes for some reason and I rarely spoke. Jack did most of the talking, enthusing about record water temperatures and amusing us with anecdotes of adolescent adventures going on each day at Poul Gorm.

It wasn't until my last evening at Myrtleville that Raphaëlle and I finally got to talk. Jack had gone to Crosshaven to collect an outboard engine straight after supper, leaving the two of us to clear the table and wash up. When we'd put the dishes away, we sat at the bay window overlooking the harbour. Outside, a shaft of evening light cut sharply through clouds on the horizon.

Raphaëlle asked me why I had ignored her since I had arrived, as though I didn't see her, as though she wasn't there. She wasn't angry, she said, she just wanted me to know that she existed, and that being Jack's girlfriend didn't mean she was invisible. I said I hadn't meant to be rude and explained that when I became absorbed by my *Priscian* research I often became oblivious to everything else. We grew more relaxed then and talked at length about what it meant to be a monk. Raphaëlle was fascinated to know what monasticism was all about. Did it mean sacrificing one's life in this world? Was the search for absolute things incompatible with living one's own desire? Did celibacy mean that desire was an obstacle to transcendence, something to be offered up for something higher? There was no hint of antagonism in Raphaëlle's questions. Just an effort to understand another way of life, one that I and many like me throughout the centuries had chosen. I did my best to answer her. I explained how the great monastic fathers – Columbanus, Bernard, Benedict – had taught that the way to perfection was a form of self-renunciation, a letting go of everything so as to enter the condition of 'grand poverty', transcendence beyond the self, obedience to a spiritual Master, a special kind of listening to a higher

Voice, one which held that true liberty comes from trusting in a Fatherhood that sustains us in our being.

Raphaëlle was intrigued but said she still couldn't understand why such a quest for perfection had so often meant treating women as temptresses, or seeing desire as a way of seducing men away from God. From Eve in Eden to the erotic apparitions of the Desert Fathers. She just couldn't comprehend, Raphaëlle said, why this world had to be seen as a deviation from God, rather than the route itself? Why women, throughout the history of religious art, were represented as imaginary fantasies rather than real beings?

She hoped I didn't mind her asking me these questions. She didn't mean to be inquisitive or personal. It was just that she'd often wondered about such things, and this was her first chance to debate with a real live monk! She laughed good-humouredly, leaning towards the table and refilling both our glasses in a semi-conscious way. There was a glow about her features as she bent forward and I noticed a tiny dark freckle just beneath her eyelid.

I didn't know how to respond to Raphaëlle's curiosity at first. I moved my mouth once or twice without saying anything, until words came. I admitted it wasn't easy for a monk to renounce his innermost desire, especially if he didn't exactly know what that desire was. Besides, a religious vocation wasn't about what one does or doesn't desire – it was about God's will. 'Not as I wilt but as Thou Wilt', as Columbanus said. That was the real difference. Learning to listen to what God wants. Learning to discern, to discriminate between God's voice and other voices.

But I felt, as I spoke, I was somehow divorced from my words.

Eventually, I stood up and looked out of the window at the crimson haze of fuschia rimming the ocean, my ribs heaving uneasily inside me. I needed to get back to my reading, I told Raphaëlle, hoping she hadn't noticed my disquiet.

Later that evening, I took a walk down to Poul Gorm and found myself thinking of Violaine and Madeleine and Mary Murphy. Above all Mary Murphy. Her arms reaching out to circle me, her face right before mine, eyes wide open even under water, and those huge white bubbles billowing up from her mouth. I discovered Raphaëlle sitting by the rocks, a cardigan over her shoulders, taking photographs of the sun going down over Ringabella. And for no reason I could explain, I immediately started telling her what had happened here with Mary Murphy all those years ago. I had never told anyone before. Not even Jack.

She said nothing for a while, then lifted her blonde fringe back from her forehead and began to speak for several minutes without stopping. She said she appreciated my confidence and felt she understood what I'd been through. She herself had seen someone almost drown the previous summer in Lac Léman, beside Geneva. She recounted the scene to me in deliberate detail.

Swimming off shore, she'd seen a man wave from a small boat and fall into the water. By the time she'd reached him he was already under water, for the third time. She dived deep until she found him. She got him back to shore with the help of other swimmers but his lungs were full, his pulse gone. Then she opened his shirt and pressed his motionless chest harder and harder until water streamed from his lips. Air rushed in to fill the vacuum and within seconds he was breathing again. Later, when he recovered, he told her how he was part of a gitan family who'd travelled up to Lake Geneva from a town in the Camargue called Saintes-Maries-de-la-Mer, following the river Rhône all the way north to its source in Lac Léman and the Grimsel pass. It was an old gitan dream, he told her, ever since the two Maries founded the town after the death of Jesus, to follow the great river back to its source in the Swiss Alps, back to the heart of an ancient continent, leaving behind the Provençale seascape of sands and wild horses and red flamingoes and sun-drenched fields of fruit trees and hibiscus . . .

Each sentence seemed to release something in Raphaëlle as she related that story, some memory that would not be forgotten, returning again and again, refusing to be silenced. And as I listened to her then, I had a sudden image of words glistening like fish in a dark sea, swimming up from some unknown blackness, open-mouthed with a message from below. But what did it mean? Why were we exchanging private memories like this? Why this moment of closeness on the eve of my departure? I did not know. All I knew was that I wanted her just then. All to myself. I wanted to take her by the elbows and kiss her mouth, open her arms and move into them.

I wanted to take Raphaëlle away from Jack.

*

There is a pounding in Jack's head, his ears. His breathing is short, as though he can't get enough air into his lungs. He sits upright in front of Sam's desk and tries several deep breaths, but each time there's a catch, an arrest, as if he's winded by what he has just read. Sam lusted after Raphaëlle! He wanted to take her from him!

Jack wonders if he shouldn't leave the journal there and go back to Raphaëlle in the guest room. Did he really need to know more? Was it right to delve further into Sam's intimate confessions and treacherous fantasies? Jack knows he shouldn't. But something irresistible compels him to read on.

Entry 22
Columbanus Abbey, 5 August, 1975

About a week after my return from Myrtleville, I had a
disturbing dream.

I was walking along a bright corridor in a large house.
There was a lake outside with lots of people dressed in white
holding a going-away party for me. A voice called from
somewhere behind a door at the end of the passageway.
'Open and come down,' it said. I descended a steep ladder
to a basement where a young man was standing in front
of a woman. The voice instructed the man to take off the
woman's clothes, to stroke her breasts and sex with his
hands. When the man was aroused and about to take her,
the voice commanded him to stop and invited me to take
his place.

The dream pierced me like a blade. I couldn't get the
images out of my mind. Black lust coursed through my
body. Especially late at night, when I felt most estranged
from God, most vulnerable to the terrible pull of want.
I called out to God to unlock the door of grace into my
underworld, to infiltrate my darkness with his saving
light, to teach me to be still. But the rush of images
kept returning, each time I tried to pray, until eventually I
wanted only to hide, tear myself away, sink into the deepest
sleep. I wanted to kill these times of nocturnal torment so
that I might be carried senseless through to morning. The
days would be easier, I knew – Matins, meals, cataloguing
and typing up the *Priscian* files, Mass, walks, Vespers, all
effortlessly rehearsed off as doing His will. But the nights
were impossible. I saw her everywhere. I was full of
wanting. Whatever happened, I had to have Raphaëlle.

Entry 23
Columbanus Abbey, August 1975-June 1976

I told Anselm about Raphaëlle, of course, confiding my dream and subsequent torments. I assumed it would be difficult, but it wasn't. Anselm's calm baffled me. He made no comment, only reminded me of the reading from Vespers that evening, the verse from Psalm 24 about the voice of the Lord showing the path to those who stray, rescuing their feet from snares, relieving the anguish of the heart. He counselled patience, discipline, more prayer. It was all part of the journey, he said. God will protect you, he added with a smile, as you write under the greenwood tree.

But the images of Raphaëlle kept coming back, again and again, no matter what I did, no matter how resolutely I wrestled and prayed, until one night I woke and found myself in a black hole. A place that was no place. No walls, no boundaries, nothing to cling to. Everything had slipped away exposing one gaping pit of emptiness. I cried out to God to rescue me from this vortex, sucking me deeper and deeper into its void. It was night but the most terrifying thing of all was that everything was white. Absolute whiteness. Absence of all colours. No colour. Blankness. No-self.

I went to Anselm and we prayed together until morning came. Later that day he came to my room with a commentary on Romans 4. He told me I was now experiencing one of the great Christian mysteries – dying unto the self – and read me the following passage: 'Faith beholds life and existence where the man of the world sees nothing but death and non-existence; and contrariwise, it sees death and non-existence; where he beholds full-blooded life. The living must die in order that the dead may be made alive. The things which are must be seen as though they were not in order that the things which are not may be called as though they were.' He told me to reflect on this and to compile an inventory of similar extracts from the Gospels and other spiritual writings over the coming months. He suggested we take time once a week to meditate together on each passage. It would be a way, he said, of developing those powers of discernment prescribed in Columbanus's rule of Discretion – 'True discretion cleaves to Christian lowliness and opens the way of perfection to Christ's true soldiers, namely by ever discerning correctly in doubtful cases'.

So over that second year of my novitiate, in addition to continuing research with Anselm on the *Priscian,* I compiled a series of 'discernment' texts. These were mainly from the Rule of Columbanus but also included passages from the Gospels, Psalms, Jeremiah, Paul and other spiritual authors. I called them 'Night Fragments' as most were recorded after Vespers and before Matins. I kept a selection of them in the form of an appendix to this journal.

Pondering these fragments more and more during the year, sometimes with Anselm, sometimes alone, I became convinced that if I could go deep enough into the void I'd learn to listen to a single voice which would reveal me to myself. The crucial task was, of course, to learn how to discern, to discriminate between the true voice of the Master and the multiple other voices that came and went, day and night, like radio signals criss-crossing in the night. And each time, after long meditation, when I prepared my soul to listen, I recited to myself Columbanus's precept on Perfection: 'Let the monk live under the discipline of one father – whose duty it belongs to fulfil what he is bidden, as Moses says, Hear, O Israel'.

As the months progressed and I began to feel more grounded I decided to send a copy of the 'Fragments' to

Raphaëlle. I suppose I wanted her to know the extremity of my struggle, to show how I was wrestling my way towards some truth. To respond, too, in some oblique fashion, to her engagement to Jack. She sent a photograph in reply. A picture she'd taken of a high wave off Poul Gorm, with these words handwritten on the back: 'We do not renounce the world to reach God: we rediscover the world in God. Deep calling on deep'. I showed it to Anselm, expecting he'd say something, but he didn't.

In early June I received word from Jack and Raphaëlle that they were taking a trip to Paris in July; they invited me to join them, if I wished, during my summer break. I mentioned it to Anselm and was surprised to hear him say it might do me good. Especially after the long winter.

Entry 24
France, 22–29 July, 1976

Entry 24 i

On 22 July we took the ferry from Rosslare to Cherbourg. It was packed: queues for everything. Restaurant, cabins, duty-free, money exchange. 'We're all Europeans now!' said Jack, mocking a recent election slogan.

We found a place in the upper deck lounge with a view of the waves. Raphaëlle sat in a lotus position with a book in front of her. The more she read that afternoon the more absorbed she became, her body so still at one point I could count the tiny tributaries of blue vein on her neck and shoulders. Her eyes were concentrated, unaware of Jack or me or anyone. Or maybe she was not so unaware? Maybe she did feel my eyes on her bare neck? Or Jack's eyes, not looking at her, looking out of the window, but watching nonetheless?

It was when Jack went to get drinks at the counter that Raphaëlle looked across at me and read a piece from her book. She spoke in careful, well-stressed English, in a low voice. One bit she read twice, holding the book out, eyes narrowing to a slight squint.

Never stay with what is like you. Never stay anywhere. When your surroundings have taken on your likeness or you yourself have grown like your surroundings, they cease to profit you. You must leave them. Take from each thing nothing but what it teaches you; and let the pleasure that streams from it drain it dry. The most beautiful thing you will know on earth is your hunger, your desire. The nomad's life is the shepherd's life

'Do you believe that?' I asked her.

'I do,' she said, returning the book to her lap.

'Why?'

'Because desire is always for something you can't have. And I think it's true that we should leave people or things as soon as they become like us, or we become like them . . .'

'. . . which makes us Irish top of your league,' Jack interposed, returning with the drinks. 'We're scattered all over the globe.'

'A migrant race!' Raphaëlle said.

'If you like,' Jack acknowledged, a little irritated for some reason. 'But it's nothing to celebrate. Most emigrants had no choice; they left because they had to. There was nothing romantic about it. No tourist itch . . .'

'That is not what I am talking about,' Raphaëlle replied, laying her open book face downwards on the table. 'I'm talking about a journey compelled by something missing inside us, a gap or hole in our lives, something we can never fill.'

'Well, maybe I just don't buy this metaphysical longing bit,' Jack said. Then he changed the subject, suggesting we go on deck to see Land's End before it disappeared.

'*Allons-y*,' rejoined Raphaëlle with a crisp smile. She put a hand on each of Jack's shoulders.

I didn't go with them, making some excuse about feeling queasy and needing sleep. But I watched Jack and Raphaëlle through the porthole as they walked together along the deck and bent over the railings. Raphaëlle kept winding her camera, taking shots of low-flying gannets and kittiwakes. She looked tall in her long pullover, pushing her blonde fringe from her eyes. Like Carlotta Valdes, I thought, peering into San Francisco Bay. Jack looked the part too, stalwart beside her, the sea wind blowing his shirt against his chest. But there was something missing. Some curious distance between Jack and Raphaëlle. Their eyes, their hands, rarely seemed to meet. Or maybe I was just imagining it. After a while, Jack left, but Raphaëlle stayed on, gazing down from the railing into the waves.

In the lounge couples compared notes on camping sites in Brittany and Spain. I stayed sitting there a while, until Jack came back to say that the Normandy coast was in sight. A thin lip of shoreline on the horizon was just visible now through the porthole; and behind it miles of expectant continent. That's how it must have seemed to the Allies, too, landing there over thirty years ago. The Longest Day. But I was thinking of other things – Raphaëlle back in her cabin, stretched on her side, a glossy knee exposed, with one arm flung behind her head, the other dangling from her bunk. I closed my eyes, several times, but the shutter would not fall inside my head. Lines from the Psalm raced through me.

Deep calling upon deep,
in the roar of waters.
Your torrents and your waves
sweep over me . . .

Entry 24 ii

'*Regardez les coccinelles!*' Raphaëlle kept saying as we stepped off the boat at Cherbourg. I wasn't sure what she was thinking about until I noticed that our arms and legs were covered in black and red wings. Swarms of tiny ladybirds.

We decided on a swim before catching the train for Paris. On our way to the seafront we grabbed a *moules frites* and jealously savoured the hundred-franc menu on display outside a chic restaurant on the promenade. Raphaëlle read each course with palate-precise relish.

— *Loup de Mer à la Braise.*
— *Bar au Fenouil.*
— *Calamar à l'Armoricaine.*
— *Feuilleté de Homard.*
— *Sorbet aux Poires.*

The seats inside were red plush, all occupied, like the restaurant scene where Scottie first saw Carlotta. Outside, the promenade was spilling over with lovers linking arms, adolescents on bicycles and gangs of small kids holding up bunches of ladybirds, like painted peanuts, singing funny verses over and over:

*J'fais pipi sur le gazon
pour embêter les coccinelles,
J'fais pipi sur le gazon,*

> *pour embêter les papillons,*
> *pipi, pipi,*
> *J'ai envie de faire pipi.*

Odours of sea wrack and sun-oil wafted from the beach and gulls cried as we swam, all three of us, through the warm water. But Jack and I did not stay long. We saw something that looked like a squid, full of purple inky stuff and long string tails. Raphaëlle laughed and kept swimming far out on her own until she was scarcely visible between the waves.

Entry 24 iii

We reached Paris late in the afternoon, left our bags at the Hôtel Alésia and took the Métro to the centre. We wandered through the Tuileries, across the Pont Neuf, and followed the quays towards the Latin Quarter. Raphaëlle, who knew the city and the language, played guide. One moment, she was utterly present, touching Jack or me on the shoulder, urging us to cross a street or pointing excitedly to some building or other. The next she was off in her own world, deep inside herself, distant, self-possessed as ever.

That evening I left Jack and Raphaëlle in a café and went to see a film. I took the Métro to Odéon but became so dazed by the swish of doors opening and shutting I overshot by two stops. From St Sulpice I walked down Rue des Canettes until I came in sight of Danton's statue – revolutionary guardian of the Odéon cinemas.

Jane Fonda was playing in a film called *The Blue Bird*. My first glimpse of Hanoi Jane since I'd joined the novitiate! Pure celluloid pleasure. It was late before I got something to eat. A small Lebanese restaurant on the corner of the Rue Mazarine. Couscous and a carafe of Sidi Brahim. The restaurant was packed, even at that hour, with Arab music phrasing a heat-haze of cramped bodies. A North African girl in a blue shirt at an opposite table caught my attention. She reminded me of Raphaëlle, only darker, thinner, smaller maybe, but the same bold concentrated gaze (as when Raphaëlle read from books or wound her camera). The girl returned my stare after a while and, defiant, didn't let go. My chest tightened like when a plane takes off. I left my food half eaten and headed back to Alésia.

It was on my way to the Métro that I passed the Rue des Quatre Vents, where Cilian had lived with Pascale Questiaux all those years ago. I suddenly thought I smelled Gauloises and overheard his voice inside my head reciting the 'Pont Mirabeau' and recounting his favourite scenes from *Quai des Brumes* and *Hôtel du Nord*, films he and Pascale must have discussed together for hours into the night. And I recalled then too, as I looked up at the line of dormer windows lighting the street, of his parting counsel to me when he left the Abbey. We were alike, he'd said, he and I: made to find ourselves in this world, not to sacrifice ourselves for the next. We'd had no communication since. I wondered what had become of him.

On the Métro back, a busker sang Joni Mitchell's 'Blue' with a Bronx accent and I wondered, for some reason, why secret hungers always come at night, in the dark, like screens flickering in pitch-black spaces. And I imagined Raphaëlle back at the hotel, in a room with open shutters, lying with Jack – her hair back, face unguarded, moving, deeply stirred, staring straight up into my brother's eyes.

Entry 24 iv

My head was splitting when Jack woke me next morning.

A white sun blazed through the window, making him look like a seraphim from one of those cheap holy pictures with shards of light shooting out on all sides. He told me that Raphaëlle and he had decided to get married. I was surprised at how surprised I was, but didn't show it. I congratulated him.

We took breakfast at a large table with a fat American hippie and three Italian students. Raphaëlle got to talking with them about an exhibition on 'Hyperrealism' at the Grand Palais. The Italians said it was extraordinary – a brilliant parody of our contemporary faith in fakes, copies, imitations; the American took an opposite view. 'Cool it, *frères*!' he kept repeating, stroking his beard with one hand and holding the collar of his bright Hawaiian shirt with the other. He introduced himself as Bill, one-time sixties Marxist from Los Angeles – 'City of the Angels where all things sing.' Hyperrealism was about capital, he insisted, both eyes dilating as he removed a pair of *Easy Rider* shades. It's a worldwide thing and knows no boundaries, turns everything into its opposite, feeds our dreams into a single dream, a silver screen of sameness . . .

I watched him do this preacher bit with Raphaëlle, his red tongue moving over a thick wet underlip. And I watched Raphaëlle respond with svelte instinct to the exchange, beads of tiny moisture glistening under her eyes, a hint of jasmine filling the air each time she turned her head. Jack made a joke then about her being 'Miss Geneva Convention', arbitrating between rival partners. The whole thing sounded like rubbish, he said. He suggested we visit the Maritime Museum in Trocadero instead; there we could see models of historic transatlantic liners on display – *Lusitania, Mauritania, QE II, Queen Mary*. But Raphaëlle had already decided. We would visit the Grand Palais.

We took the Métro to Concorde and walked up le Cours La Reine. I stayed several steps behind and watched Jack take Raphaëlle's arm to cross the road. A sharp blade of light glanced off her shoulder when she turned towards him. I had never seen her look so good. The Grand Palais loomed into sight like some overgrown glasshouse. The tree-lined pavement in front milled with buskers, mime-artists, and food vendors. Inside, Raphaëlle asked for directions and led me and Jack through the maze of corridors and stairs to the Hyperrealism exhibition on the top floor. It was like following Carlotta Valdes into the gallery of paintings.

Facing us as we entered the exhibit space was a pop parody of a blonde vamp: head on pillow, she stared out from her acrylic den, a bubble caption floating from pouting lips – 'Good Morning Darling'. Behind it stretched a long line of Warhol seriographs, multiple faces of media stars from Marilyn Monroe to Jackie Kennedy. Norma Jean played like a wild card between JFK and Bobby, exchanged from one to the other in the game of desire. Maybe Jackie felt the same? Like all those Warhol faces. Looking in several directions at once. Double lives with double names. Jackie and Jacqueline. Marilyn and Norma Jean. Jack and John.

Then Raphaëlle whisked us into an adjoining salle full of giant pastiches of David's 'Marat', Rembrandt's 'Jacob', Ligozzi's 'Tobie et l'ange'; and beside them looming bill-board parodies of Pall Mall commercials, Diner burgers and Budweiser beer. Raphaëlle read something aloud from the French catalogue about us all now living in a labyrinth, where representations rule the world, where no one can tell copies from originals. But I didn't quite understand what she was getting at. Her countenance remained as elusive as the fleeting Warhol faces on the walls around us.

Jack and I stood behind Raphaëlle going down the stairs. It was so high at the top I could see most of the city stretched out beneath us through the glass dome. Upturned, upcoming faces glided past, but Raphaëlle was inviolate as if some white cocoon of air had wound around her. I fixed my gaze on Raphaëlle's back, her hair tied up in a spiral curl exposing her sallow neck, the camera slung across her back and a thin line of purple strap running from shoulder-blade to shoulder-blade.

My head became cloudy, a dizzy ache nagging inside. I couldn't look down any more, and couldn't look away. I feared I would fall, like when I was on the chairoplanes with Jack at the Merries in Crosshaven, waiting to get off, counting the seconds before the reeking oily machine would crank to a halt and release its charges back to earth. I longed to reach ground level, to be out of that glass maze, to step from those two-way stairs on to open streets.

Entry 24 v

The return journey was the worst. A band played on the upper deck of the *St Patrick* and Raphaëlle insisted on dancing. Flushed and giddy, she dragged Jack on to the polished circle, clinging to his arms as she spun around the small space. She trod the floor sure-footed, her Marianne Faithfull fringe up from her forehead, making her eyes alert and bold as she abandoned herself to the music. Once more she was in possession of her powers the very moment she let go.

Jack sat down after a bit but Raphaëlle wanted to go on. She insisted I dance with her; so did Jack, making some crack about novices learning to jive like David before the Ark. Taking my hand, Raphaëlle guided me deftly through the maze of crowded tables to the dance ring in the middle of the lounge. *O Israel! You shall take your tambourines and go forth in the dance of the merrymakers!* It was a fast waltz and she drew in close after a few seconds, gripping my shoulder and letting her body be taken by the pace. *Put bracelets on your arms, earrings in your ears, a crown upon your head, queen among the nations!* We wheeled around faster and faster, turning and returning in a whirl of light. *Let us anoint our heads with oils and mix wines until the cup flows!* Background details of people and things spun into single motion, like spoked wheels revolving at speed. And soon everything turned so fast I found myself staring into Raphaëlle's eyes to keep from falling, and Raphaëlle stared back at me like a blazoned icon, immobile against the whirring background – frameless, gold-leaf, elusive, free. And I knew that if I looked away I'd fall, for there was only Raphaëlle's gaze now, all others ceasing to exist. There were only her eyes now, the dilated centre of my gravity, each of us seeing what the other was seeing. I was sure of it. I could see it now, couldn't I? Raphaëlle had smiley eyes.

We returned to our table after that dance. Jack ordered a last round of drinks. A calm stole over Raphaëlle's features and they went blank; she was somewhere else and then she was back, looking intently as if she'd never been away.

Jack and Raphaëlle went to their cabin shortly afterwards. I went to mine. But I didn't sleep. I couldn't. I lay on my bed, turned the lights off and pulled the blanket over my head. I tried to think of nothing, but faces began flashing through my brain, one after another – Carlotta and Madeleine, Jackie Kennedy and Marilyn Monroe, Mary Murphy and Violaine, Marianne Faithfull and Maggie Kiely, the Arab girl and the Angel of St Gallen. And recurring through them all, again and again, like a warp and weft through the threading, spinning images, her face, the visage inscribed in my body and soul since that first day in Myrtleville.

I buried my head beneath the pillow but the rasp of the engine deep within the ship kept me awake, a guttural whisper inside my head. Raphaëlle was trying to tell me something, I was sure. The reading from the book. The paintings. The dance. Signs, signals, semaphore. But too oblique. Too unspoken. One moment, she was utterly there, then she was gone, without a word. That singular autonomy that seemed at times so like indifference. I was certain she was saying something, something about my vocation. I could almost hear her voice: What do you want, Sam? What do you really want? I imagined her asking me that. But why? To find out who I really was? To save me? To seduce me? Then her voice inside me died away and images returned.

I imagined more, much more. Raphaëlle coming towards my cabin and me getting up and opening the door. Taking her by the hands then and drawing her in where it is dark. I stand close to her and say she is a great dancer and she laughs but doesn't say anything. She doesn't see anything either, it is so dark. But I know her eyes are looking into mine, her mouth opening on to mine, her breath quick and tight like mine; and I know we will kiss within seconds and take each other by the elbows and go towards my bed, not saying a word, in any language, but letting our bodies speak for us, as in the dance. Forgetting ourselves as we become each other.

And as we lose ourselves, we know that we are losing Jack too, both of us, betraying him, behind his back, breaking his trust as we knew we would, from the beginning, from the time we met in Myrtleville, sensing what would come to pass — inevitably, recurringly, like sea creatures swallowing webbed tails in the margins of illuminated manuscripts, tongues turning on words that cannot be spoken, stories telling stories about stories, flocks of voices circling around things that cannot be remembered. For as we lie inside each other, we cannot remember anything, our bodies twisting in the dark, returning to that unnameable place where selves pass in and out of the other, back and forth, up and down, like a meeting of rivers, a crossing of wings, a feeling of angels.

Then I imagined Raphaëlle looking at her watch and saying that she must go, back to her bed, to her cabin, before Jack wakes and finds her gone. And she goes and I get up then, after she leaves, the scent of deep sea and jasmine still lingering; and I write her a letter, a secret letter saying she must never tell Jack what happened, that it must always be our secret, our forbidden secret. For it was always forbidden, I explain to her. I was always one too many, from the beginning, the one who always wanted more than he could have, who always wanted what the other had, more than the other had, more than his brother had, the one who always got it too, who got away with everything. The one who got away.

*

Jack throws the journal to the floor and stands upright. He glares about the room in a dazed, half-conscious way, taking in nothing in particular. There is a grinding in his stomach. He is full of self-reproach. How could he not have seen it? How could he never have guessed, all that time, throughout their trip to France? Sam had been fantasizing about her day and night. And he'd suspected nothing. Maybe it was because Sam was so close that he'd never actually known him, never really questioned him about himself, never assumed there could be so much hidden, so much devious imagining. Even Sam's desires were counterfeit. Mimetic. Stolen metaphors. Projections. Imitations. Likenesses. Every woman Sam desired was 'like' someone else, never herself. Sam didn't love Raphaëlle, he loved a fantasy. Sex in the head. He'd never touch the real Raphaëlle. He'd never take her away. But, of course, he'd never take her. Sam was dead.

Jack sits back in the chair, sobs breaking from him now, almost unbeknownst to himself, but no tears. He bends towards the ground where Sam's journal lies and lifts it up on to the desk.

Entry 25
Columbanus Abbey, August 1976 – June 1977

Entry 25 i

This year has taught me that my struggle with Raphaëlle has been given for a purpose. It is God's way of reaching into the midnight of my soul. Even my work on the *Priscian* seems meaningless at times. As if Raphaëlle had been sent as some riddling angel to divert me from my task. I see her face on every page, her undimmed stare assaulting me through the eyes of every icon in this Abbey. The sharp tang of her otherness floods my senses like some mockery of want. The more desperately I seek her behind my imagining, the more imaginary she becomes. By sheer intensity, desire dissolves what it desires. Ravenous thirst robbing the taste of drink. A drowning man clutching his rescuer so hard he can't be saved. Cries so frantic they deafen the voice they cry for. I pray, but there is no answer.

This is the time of desire, the time of compulsion, the time of lies. Anselm is right, I know he is, when he says that to flee this midnight torment would be to renounce the struggle. My life with God must penetrate this darkness, must answer desire, speak the unspeakable, descend into the pit and open it to God's radiating presence – Only by doing these things can I hope to tell His voice from the others.

Entry 25 ii

I have been having a curious dream these last months,

different versions of the same scene. I am travelling on a boat and a beautiful lady tosses coins to boys swimming in the water. She shows a sovereign to me, then casts it into the water. I dive in from the boat, swimming down deeper and deeper until I eventually catch the coin glistening in the dark. Then I begin to swim upwards towards the surface, fathom by fathom, closer and closer to the light, but I don't seem able to reach it. I am running out of air. My lungs are bursting.

I sent the dream to Raphaëlle but she did not reply. I showed it to Anselm in his office the same day but he was unperturbed. He said it was just another signpost on the journey through the night. The important thing was to go with it and listen, emptying the self until some new life came to fill the void. *Kenosis*. Just as the Saviour emptied himself to become like man, we must empty ourselves to become like God. *Mortificatio* was how St Columbanus described it in his Rule, he reminded me, taking the *Sancti Columbani Opera* from his shelves and opening it at section ix. But you can only complete this struggle, this purgation, Anselm explained, if there is something to struggle with. You can only empty yourself of desire if you desire. Only then are you able to wrestle with your demon, retrieve its name and give it back to God.

I was bewildered by this turn of argument. But that was always the way with Anselm. You could never predict what he'd say next, but knew that he was right once he'd said it. I was beginning to see new connections. The two kinds of struggle – inner and outer, quest of self and quest of Logos – were not, it was now transpiring, as divergent as they seemed. Anselm advised me to devote the rest of the Paschal period to some remaining sections of my *Priscian* research. Out of this concentrated discipline of inquiry, this renewed vigour of questioning, something would emerge, he said, gazing benignly from behind his wide oak desk, some special alertness to a higher cause which would steel my spirit and prepare it for the last step in the itinerary.

From February to mid-March and then again from April to the end of May, I applied myself with rigorous diligence to further work on the *Priscian* edition. My scrupulous studies and readings took the form of nine final *quaestions* which I compiled in the following order and presented to Anselm:

i.   Are there residues of pre-Christian Irish culture still in evidence in the *Gall Priscian* – references to Brigid by Máel-Patricc – or are these merely playful allusions?

ii. Did the reformist evangelism of the *Céle Dé* reform, epitomized by the *Gall Priscian*, have something to do with the despatch of three of Ireland's most outstanding scholars to the three Kingdoms of Carolingian Europe in the ninth century – Eriugena to King Charles the Bald of the Western Kingdom, Moengal to Emperor Lothar of the Middle Kingdom, Sedulius Scotus to Emperor Ludwig of the Eastern Kingdom?

iii. Does not the discovery of the missing *Priscian* index, collecting the fragmented Gaelic glosses into a single folio, not confirm the suggestion of a single guiding authorship and single theological intent – namely, that the scattered marginal letterings contain a system of cyphers pointing to a unifying Logos? The way of Perfection prescribed in section X of the Rule of Columbanus?

iv. Is the lost 'Voice of God' sought after by European scriptoria from Castledermot to Constantinople not the Voice of Yahweh's secret alphabet mentioned in the Book of Creation, known in Hebrew as the *Sefer Yetsirah*? If so, is it not a Voice of oneness pre-existing time, history, difference, desire?

v. Why were the Irish scribes so obsessed with this particular line from the *Priscian* – 'Philosophers define voice as very fine air which has been struck or as a sound which eventually strikes the ear'? Why their enigmatic gloss, inscribed in both Gaelic and Latin between these lines: *'Citabiat chlúasa/cado, accido/vox'*, meaning roughly 'what ears perceive/fall, fall upon/ voice'. Why the play on fall/fall upon? A reference to the Fall of the Divine Word into history with Adam and Eve? Or the Fall of language into further division at Babel? Or the Fall of St Gallus himself into blindness when he 'fell upon' the site of his scriptorium?

vi. Is there a system of correspondences concealed within the two Gaelic verses, habitually dismissed as linguistic exotica by commentators of the *Gall Priscian*:

A row of trees surrounds me, a blackbird sings to me
Above my lined parchment, birds chant
Highest of all the cuckoo in his grey cloak
Truly may God protect me, for well do I write
Under the Greenwood tree.

I do not fear because the wind is fierce tonight
It ruffles the bright mane of the sea
I do not fear the crossing of the calm sea
by the fierce warriors of Lothlind.

Are not the grey-cloaked angels, chanting the Voice of God, being asked to protect the scribes from the world of chaos which lies beyond the greenwood scriptorium (Castledermot?) – a world typified by the flashing turbulence of the sea and its barbarous invaders? Was it such foreign invaders that first drove Gallus and Columbanus from Ireland at the beginning of the seventh century?

vii. Is it not revealing that the words used to describe this sea of chaos – *glégorm/glas/glaucus* – are also used to denote the colour of the scribe's ink: *dig ndaélda do dub glégorm* (a beast-coloured draught of bright-blue ink)? Is this not a version of the mystical maxim: near the poison you will find the cure? Sacred poison (ink) against evil poison (sea)? Perhaps even a poison that cures our forgetfulness of the Voice and opens our ears to its unifying Word? Yet another allusion to the Doctrine of Discretion taught by Gallus and Columbanus?

viii. Does the final gloss in the *Priscian* index – *ad trans-migrationem Babylonis* – not refer to the Babylonian migration which, the Bible tells us, was fourteen generations after David and fourteen generations before Christ? Is the transmission of the Word from generation to generation being compared here to the transmission of coded letters from manuscript to manuscript, transferring the Voice of Genesis from the beginning to the end of history, as signalled in the sermons of Columbanus?

ix. What, finally, does the rediscovered index tell us of the enigmatic 'fall' of Gallus – recorded in the *Casus Sancti Galli* at St Gallen? Does it reveal the meaning of Gallus's life? Does it disclose some divine plot behind the various episodes in the spiritual history of St Gallen outlined above? A meaning behind the meaning? *Casus* as 'Life' or 'Fall' or accidental 'event' (case)? How tell the difference? How discern? For as Columbanus teaches: 'Discretion got its name from discerning . . . Righteous Abel chose the good, but unrighteous Cain fell upon evil . . . True discretion opens the way of Perfection to Christ's true soldiers, namely by ever discerning correctly in doubtful cases' (*Sancti Columbani Opera: Regulae* viii, x–xi)

In early June Anselm called me to his office and congratulated me on my considerable progress. It was now time, he announced, after our countless consultations and discussions, to make a visit to St Gallen itself. We would leave during the annual novitiate break in July, extending our stay a few days into August to allow for proper examination of the recently discovered Index to the *Gall Priscian*. We were approaching, he believed, a decisive moment.

As I knew that Jack and Raphaëlle were planning a visit to Raphaëlle's family in Switzerland, I asked Anselm if they might accompany us for part of the way. Besides, something in me wanted Anselm to meet Raphaëlle; and to my surprise he readily agreed, suggesting we could all drive together as far as St Gallen. Jack and Raphaëlle might even stay on at the Klosterhof a day or two, if they wished, before going on to Geneva.

THE LIFE OF TOBIAS

PART FIVE

'It is for travellers to hasten to their homeland, likewise their part is anxiety upon the roadway, and in their homeland peace. Then let us, who are on the way, hasten home; for our whole life is like the journey of a single day . . . Let us place our desires above for the fatherland is there where our Father is. He is everywhere by virtue of his power and he is deeper than the ocean. God remains invisible; for He is greater than what could be seen entire, and greater than all things, for He created all of nothing . . .'

The Works of St Columbanus, Instructio VIII, 1. AD 612

$\int$

Entry 26 i

We arrived at St Gallen around 8 p.m. on the evening of 27 July. Anselm's car slowed to a crawl in the streets which were jammed with traffic and locals suspending banners from window embrasures indented with small wooden carvings. Holiday-makers poured in and out of the taverns and boutiques. Swiss Independence Day, Raphaëlle remembered, was less than a week away. And then, as we edged into the Blumenberg Platz, we finally saw it – the Abbey of St Gall – dominating the whole town with its twin copper spires reaching into the sky. *'Villa Sancti Galli!'* shouted Anselm, raising his two large hands in the air and banging them down on the steering wheel. His first time back to the Alma Mater in twelve years.

It was difficult not to share in Anselm's enthusiasm. It was infectious – the way his face filled with memory and quiet satisfaction, the way his eyes washed over every detail of landscape and architecture surrounding us, as we passed through the suburbs to the centre of the town. But Raphaëlle kept to herself. The three-day journey through France had not been easy. Anselm had insisted on following much of the original itinerary of Gallus and Columbanus eastwards, stopping off in the monastic settlements of Luxeuil, Annegray and Bregenz on the way. It was part of what he called an 'anamnetic pilgrimage'. One in which I and Jack could join him, after all he'd imparted to us as boarders, but not Raphaëlle. She was travelling home, after all, and each detour seemed to press further on her patience. From my front seat beside Anselm I caught several glimpses of her in the rear-view mirror, seated in the back, head leaning out of the window, the passing wind blowing at her hair and preventing her listening to Anselm's recollections. It was even more noticeable at table, though, in the small cafés or village hotels we stopped in: Raphaëlle would regard Anselm silently when he wasn't looking, as if trying to get at something behind his words, something he wasn't saying. They rarely engaged in conversation directly, and on the few occasions they did, the exchanges were short and without consequence. It wasn't a question of ostensible aggression, or unpleasantness. Just a general ungainliness, a pronounced reserve, as one sometimes witnesses when two people, who've heard much about each other from mutual acquaintances, get together for the first time. But this was more, one felt, than accumulated expectation or tacit assumption. There was a deep wariness behind the fascination. Anselm and Raphaëlle seemed to know at once too much and too little about each other.

Anselm had booked rooms for us in the Abbey guest house. We were met by Doctor Klaus, a wide-shouldered man with a thick-set neck, who welcomed Anselm like a long-lost brother. Anselm introduced Jack and Raphaëlle, then me. 'The *Priscian* Index, of course!' replied Klaus, pinning me with the fire of his grey eyes and inviting us all for a late supper in a restaurant in the square adjoining the Klosterhof. From our table, we could see the narrow lit streets of the town below us uncoil like luminous worms. In the dark air above us little black things darted back and forth about our heads. Bats? Swifts? Why not angels? Jack volunteered mockingly, in no mood for guessing games. In fact, Jack was in no mood for anything that night but drinking. He summoned one of the waitresses, ordered a large carafe of red and proposed a rhetorical toast to St Gallus – 'bringer of light and love to the belly of darkest Europe!' He then proceeded to observe that Swiss menus (written in three national tongues – French, German and Italian) were worse than multiple-choice tests! You start with French entrées (always taste better in French), get full on Tyrol pastas and end up with vertigo over German pastries! After a few more drinks, he tried to persuade Raphaëlle to join him in a polka played by a brass band at the opposite end of the square, but she declined. She was as intrigued as I by the conversation taking place at table between Anselm and Klaus.

Jack turned away at the mention of the *Priscian*, this time as at other times during this journey. It was as if he couldn't bring himself to rejoin the mystic hunt ever since he had left his own vocation behind him. When he observed Anselm's intensity, he couldn't help a hint of pain crossing his face, his very disavowal of interest betraying a lingering, unacknowledged attachment. Now, finding himself disconsolate witness to our impassioned exchange, Jack withdrew discreetly from the table and headed towards a nearby bar. I knew Jack regretted having come.

Dr Klaus informed us in excellent English of his work as curator of the St Gallen Archives, originally owned by the monastic order who ran the Abbey for centuries until it was largely secularized in the last century. His speciality was medieval paleography, the subject of his doctoral thesis at Zurich University before he took up his post at St Gallen twenty years ago. He had a chalky face, pocked with little swollen veins and encircled by a kempt, clipped beard. He talked at gunfire speed, when he got into his stride, his bald head bobbing away with delight as he traded opinions with Anselm about the current standing of different language schools – Geneva, Prague, Bologna, Paris. He never could abide Saussure and all that structuralist stuff, he swore with a staccato laugh. The idea that words relate to other words, not things! That language refers only to itself! That signs circulate between speakers like women between members of a tribe! Nonsense! As if letters were mere tokens of exchange – commodities, currencies! Klaus grew flushed as he went on, casting short, sharp, knowing glances in Anselm's direction.

Of course it was ridiculous, Anselm agreed, sitting forward in his chair, shrugging the lassitude of the long journey from his drooping shoulders. He vehemently defended the idea of a universal Logos capable of absorbing the cosmos into itself. A belief as old as the Church Doctors, and older, he recalled. The world as text. Nature as Book of the Universe. *Liber Mundi*. All this talk nowadays about an ideal language of structures and forms, he smiled knowingly, was just a return to the Middle Ages. A theology of the Word – without God? It could go nowhere!

Klaus greeted every phrase uttered by Anselm with a fixed grin. He removed his wire-rimmed glasses each time he listened, putting them back on again when it was his turn to speak. He never actually got beyond his hors d'oeuvre, so engrossed was he by the exchange. It was when he got to the theory of the Perfect Language, however, that he really came into his own, rumpling his eyebrows into a fuzz of intensity.

The age-old quest for a perfect tongue, Klaus explained, echoing disquisitions I'd heard over the years, invariably harked back to some ancient language. In the early Middle

Ages, his own research made clear to him, countless monks devoted their lives to the search for the lost letters of Genesis – what came to be known as the 'Adamic Grammar'. This was said to be the secret alphabet of Creation which Yahweh used to make the world, to converse with Adam in the cool of the morning. But the Grammar was forfeited after the Fall and lost for ever after Babel. Many mystical minds – kabbalists, alchemists, gnostics – became crazed in quest of hidden ways back to the Lost Language. But no one ever managed to retrieve those First Words of naming, that pristine condition when each sign fitted its ordained thing, when the tongues of God and man were one, when God named Adam and Adam named everything else. No one ever succeeded in returning to that time before time, the time before Eve and the serpent tempted the First Man to know evil as well as good, death as well as life, lies as well as truth, to know opposites – the time, in short, before the One of Eden fell into the many of history. After that, unities of name and thing were broken irretrievably, each sign came to mean different things, and split tongues crossed and criss-crossed in a manic wrestle of words – what the Bible called Babel.

Klaus finished his lecture and laughed, delighted with himself. Anselm nodded with pale, level eyes, as if he had nothing more to add. But Raphaëlle had some questions.

'Why did people keep on hunting for the perfect Grammar,' she asked, 'if it was lost for ever?'

Anselm seemed not to hear her speak, but Klaus relished the challenge, his grin so wide it sent lines racing across his face like a white page breaking into squiggles.

'Because some ancient commentaries on the Bible spoke of Yahweh regretting his expulsion of Adam and sending down an angel to his descendants, Abraham and Shem, bearing a secret Book of Creation. This was believed to contain a coded script for the lost alphabet.' Klaus moved his hands animatedly as he spoke. 'Whoever found the key would recover the Grammar of Genesis, undo the legacy of Babel and bring back fallen creatures to the Logos of perfection!'

'How?' Raphaëlle focused her eyes into a quizzical squint.

Klaus paused. A half-smile creased the corner of his mouth. He continued, 'That's what certain people have been trying to find out all these centuries. But the greatest apprentices to signs never got to the secret. Rabbis tried it with Golem tales, using parchment sequences of words called *shems* to make creatures out of nothing, like Yahweh first made Adam. Neo-Platonists tried it with crypted doctrines of descent and ascent, emanation and return. Alchemists searched endlessly for the hidden formula of the philosopher's stone. But none of them *got* it. Not a single one. The closer they approached the more it eluded them. They couldn't get back before Babel. Some hints and guesses maybe. An odd trace here or there. That's all.'

'What sort of trace?' Raphaëlle asked, her face set.

'We won't go into that here,' Klaus chuckled. He looked across at Anselm, then back at Raphaëlle. 'But I'll tell you this,' he added, lowering his voice as he poked his head forward in a gesture so sudden it spread ripples down his neck. 'The *Priscian* Index may have something to tell us.'

Then he laughed aloud, raising his glass from the table and leaning back in his chair.

Entry 26 ii

Next morning, Anselm woke me early to visit the archives. That's where the *Gall Priscian* was kept, in the old scriptorium library housing the famous Irish collection – the *Libri Scottici Scripti*. Anselm led the way along a series of corridors full of illuminated display cases, portraits, curved domes and panelled shelves. There was a polished smell about the place. We passed the Stiftsbibliothek or main library which Anselm informed me contained 1725 volumes. Amongst them, some of the most celebrated texts of ancient learning – Boethius's *De Consolatione*, Capella's *De Nuptiis Philologiae et Mercurii*, the ten-volume *Cursus Theologicus*. We then traversed a vast double-choir church and adjoining cloister before reaching the manuscript room at the other end of the Klosterhof. Approaching the archive, I asked Anselm about the curious wooden engravings lining the outer wall. 'The St Gallen Sibyls,' Anselm replied matter-of-factly, indicating little interest in pursuing the matter. He opened the door then and ushered me into the room with his outstretched hand,

There was a smell of beeswax and leather preservative inside. Anselm weaved his way about the low-ceilinged space like someone returning to a former dwelling. Nothing seemed unfamiliar. The tunnel-vault roof with three pairs of lunettes, the round-arched windows to west and south, the free-standing cabinets with double doors and stained walnut inlays, the wooden moulds veneered with spiral and foliage tendrils; and, of course, the tall bound volumes of the manuscripts themselves, numbered from 1 to 560 and displayed in long cased shelves with holy figures carved on them – Tobit, Isaac, Samson, Simeon, Gallus. 'You must be blind before you read,' said Anselm softly, reciting the inscription over the bookshelves. He surveyed the illuminated parchments, one after another, caressing each of them with masterly eyes as though they were supplicant creatures kept down with clasps, obedient to his gaze. He inclined his body towards them, like someone relishing longed-for prey. Then we came upon it, at last, in the corner of the scriptorium, the cased manuscript of the recently discovered Index.

Here was the supplement to the *Priscian* I'd heard so much about, speculated over all those months, surmising multiple hypotheses about its origins and ends. Here it was, the original document laid out before me. A shrivelled, creased folio, purplish in colour and lined with minuscule squiggles. Zeros, crosses, tendrils and circles jostled into sequences that made up sentences, each following the other from the top of the parchment to the bottom. Exposed under covered glass like that, the serried lines looked like hordes of little ink-stained monks leading each other in a manic dance.

'Why this particular sequence?' I asked.

'That's what we are here to find out,' Anselm replied.

We both fell silent then and continued to gaze upon the parchment for what seemed like ages, scrutinizing each line, stroke by stroke, letter by letter, gloss by gloss. Somewhere above us a window pane rattled and I could hear stray dry branches creaking on the trees outside in the cloisters. An uncanny peace invaded the scriptorium. For a few minutes I felt I understood the motto of St Gallen. *Verbum Domini Manet Internum.* The Word of God resides within.

Klaus joined us later in the morning and rehearsed the basics of the Index for me. He hunched over the folio like a cartographer over a map, explaining how each line of cursive lettering made up a gloss from the original *Priscian*, subsequently transcribed on to this sewn parchment. The real challenge was, of course, to find the *logic of the sequence*! As he spoke, up close like that, his breath was acrid, and his eyes protruded behind the smoked glass of his lenses, a funny white cloud behind the left iris making it opaque and stony-looking. Between each rapid explanation, Klaus would hook his bearded head forward like a boxer butting, giving added force to his expression. But in spite of his physical repulsiveness he made me marvel at how that one single page listed all the marginalia of the *Priscian* Grammar, its errant inessentials and addenda, its idiosyncratic afterthoughts jotted between lines of the 240 pages of manuscript, scattered whisper-thoughts collated on to a single parchment sheet. Some of the old Irish scribes were out of their minds when they entered these scribblings, Klaus averred, if one is to believe the Gaelic admissions of all-night drinking bouts inscribed in the margins – *lathairt!* But that's just it, exclaimed Klaus, brightening, that was their trick! To make the marginal jottings *seem* like throw-aways! To make the added index *appear* irrelevant, dispensable, a mere extravagance! That's how the scribes of the *Priscian* sought to cipher their message, cover their code, conceal all access to the perfect language! That's it! One page of scribble holding the key to the entire Grammar!

Klaus rounded his phrase off with theatrical relish, raising his white hands in the air and bringing the tips of his fingers down on the edge of the display case, carefully, pianissimo, with a smothered, falsetto laugh.

Entry 26 iii

When I got back to the guest house, I found Jack nursing a hangover. Raphaëlle had gone for a walk in the hills behind the Abbey, he said, to a small lake called the Blauloch. Jack was in no mood to hear the latest on the *Priscian*, so I left him in his room and went down to the receptionist in the main hall for directions to the lake.

I walked at a brisk pace through the Borromeo Gate of the Abbey down through the Gallustrasse. The spacious Gallusplatz was crammed with visitors sitting under bright canopies sipping drinks in the afternoon heat. From there, I took a short cut up through Moosbruggstrasse leading to the Stadt-Park at the foot of the hill. My pace quickened, until I eventually found myself striding rapidly between exposed trunks of oaks and sycamore, the brown-tiled roofs of St Gallen disappearing further and further behind me. I paused on the crest of the first hill to take in the plunging view of the townscape – the Altstadt below bristling with narrow buildings extending into dormer roofs, curved turrets and coloured window frames, tiny people milling through the streets. The sun slipped behind a cloud then and the town beneath seemed to shrink and go dark. I turned back upon my path, lifting my eyes towards the fuzzy evergreens above me, like so many outstretched fingers pointing to mountain ranges beyond with yellowing summits and brilliant surfaces. For a moment just then, I thought of Gallus and Columbanus all those centuries ago looking on to these same heights, so much higher and harsher than the gentle native slopes of Bangor and Antrim they had once strolled upon and left behind, master and disciple, dreaming their dream of a journey to the centre of Europe, to the *axis mundi*, carrying the flame of the unifying Word back to the heart of divided tribes. Yes, I thought of those two missionary brothers leading their troop of black-robed disciples, bedraggled after months of journeying by foot and sea, river and mountain; and I imagined them still chanting their *Credo in Unum Deum*, over and over, heroically staving off hunger, sickness, sleeplessness, cold, their heavy hide codicils and satchelled psalters hoisted high upon their shoulders, eyes still brimming with undimmed expectation.

Now there were only evergreens and redwoods about me, tall and bold. *Sempervirens*. Survivors through the ages, as Anselm always said. Huge domes of green filtering light through staggered branches down on to a patchwork quilt of clearings. But the more I climbed into those Berneggwald hills, the less I thought of Anselm, Gallus, Columbanus.

Surrounding trees dissolved into a blur the faster I went, as visions of Raphaëlle came swimming into my mind. Straw-haired, stripped down to the flesh, kneeling beside that pool high in the hills. Green eyes shut, she takes me to her. I grip her legs in the crux of my arms and raise her on to me, waist-high, coaxing her open until she breaks into a quiet moan and enfolds me. And I can suddenly feel every inch of that eager-bellied, ochre body of hers, yielding to me, yielding shamelessly, fierce and abandoned. And though we know we must cease now, before someone finds us, before Jack comes, before Anselm comes, we take one more moment of pleasure, stealing one last caress from each other's furtive bodies, lingering to a shiver.

I was close to the place now. *Das Blauloch*. I hit upon a rivulet, about two miles above the Berneggwald, and kept to the small track running upstream from one pool to the next, each higher than the other, and deeper too it seemed, more difficult to pass with branches protruding from the surrounding foliage on to the hard granite boulders paving the stream on either side. And the closer I got the louder my heart beat as I imagined Raphaëlle diving from a high stone into the water and waiting for me there, under water, her arms reaching out to circle me, eyes wide open, even under water, and no sound, only bubbles, huge white bubbles, billowing up from her blue mouth, like gibsails in a wind.

As I clambered over the last high rock, I finally glimpsed her clothes and camera piled in a heap beside the plunging dip of the pool, her blue vest and jeans lying on top. And I could hear her voice too now, rising above the splashing, in a high-pitched cry. I raced through the bushes fronting the pool, the white enclosing trees sharp and close, the undergrowth of brown and sooty ash giving off strong smells of earth. And brushing aside a cluster of briars, I could see her at last, Raphaëlle, head rising above the water, neck bared, shaking long wet hair wildly back and forth in a spray of laughter. But she was not alone. There were others swimming in the water beside her. Young adolescents, about a dozen of them, up from the town no doubt, diving in at the deep edge, scampering over the rocks, sunbathing on the flat upper ledge.

I looked at Raphaëlle and she looked back, smiling, like a stranger, off-handedly, through steady, intelligent eyes. Could she see into me, I wondered; could she? Could she see the desire inside, still flaming, before the shutter went down? She saw through me, I think. I think she did.

Angel of Bethesda, stirring the pool? Calling me? To heal? To drown?

Entry 26 iv

Raphaëlle seemed giddy after her swim. She laughed fitfully to herself several times as she dried her hair with her towel, a fan of tiny wrinkles spreading out from her eyes across her soft brown face. Her arms were brown too, taut, long and brown, as she tucked her togs into her suede sack and held up her camera.

'*Sois naturel, Sam!*' she said, and clicked.

On the walk down through the Berneggwald, Raphaëlle told me new things about St Gallen, things Anselm or Klaus had never mentioned. Its visual heritage, especially. Raphaëlle explained how she'd spent the early part of the morning looking into the Abbey's collections of paintings and engravings, classified exhibits she'd originally studied in detail for her Art and Design course in Geneva. Blindness, she explained to me, was a recurring motif in many of the works. And she was convinced this had something to do with the fact that Gallus himself lost his sight at the very spot on which the Klosterhof was built – thirteen hundred years ago. The Swiss locals, she'd learned, referred to Gallus's fall as *ein Fingerzeig Gottes*. As if God himself had lowered a heavenly finger and tripped him up! Raphaëlle laughed at that, her features live and frank. She paused for a moment, clasping the strap of her camera and slinging it casually back over her shoulder.

As we descended further down the path, Raphaëlle described some of the monastery's portraits of the saint's famous fall. I was puzzled and told her so. Why had a place founded on the loss of sight given rise to so many blueprints for a Perfect Vision? The Carolingian plan for the Perfect Library? The Notker variations on a Perfect Scale? The astronomical formulae for a Perfect Cosmos? And, above all, the relentless hunt, century after century, for the Perfect Grammar to found all grammars, the key to the secret Word of Genesis? How were these quests of Perfect Vision made possible by a *loss* of vision? What could it mean?

'It depends what you mean by vision,' Raphaëlle replied. And when I had no answer to that, she suggested I visit the Gallus Chapel with her when I got back, the oratory where the saint's life was recounted in a series of portraits suspended on the roof and walls.

Back in the Klosterhof, Raphaëlle led me through the whitewashed arches and corridors of the west wing, past the double-choir church and former prior's residence, to the Gallus Chapel at the centre of the building. Before entering, however, Raphaëlle gestured to a line of sibyls etched along the outer wall, similar to those outside the archive, but with a phrase from Solomon underneath: *Nigra sum sed pulchra.* We stood there for a moment to take them in. Beaked beauties with long, webbed tongues, cloven feet and legs all covered in hairy scales. Thirteen forbidden prophetesses from different parts of the world – Erythrea, Hellespont, Sheba, Cuma – reputed to have spoken in multiple tongues. Their mouths were cleft, their limbs forked and monstrously twisted. The celibate scribes were unable, it seems, to accept that women too had 'visions', so they banished them to a hinterland of forbidden forms, obscene images to be cast aside as they entered their chapel and scriptorium each morning. Only by renouncing the power of the outer eye could the inner voice be heard, God's voice, the voice 'residing within'. Just like the motto on the door said.

I watched Raphaëlle carefully as she explained these things to me, fascinated by her sheer force of concentration. She hardly moved, her hair tied up at the back, exposing pale ears dimpled at the tips like indentations on the rims of shells. She seemed back in her element, like someone stiff-limbed becoming suddenly lithe in water. And as she gazed up at those sibyls, pointing to each one, I noticed dark rivulets of down swim like tiny seaweed along the vertebrae of her neck. Her high cheeks seemed to change colour slightly as her voice quickened, her skin turning inky-mauve for a moment, drawing light in rather than giving it out. A shadow veiled her countenance as though she were carrying precious things inside her. And as I observed her there, surrounded by her troupe of dazzling sibyls, at the entrance to the Gallus Chapel, I thought of Carlotta Valdes staring at portraits of her former self on the gallery wall. But why was Raphaëlle so eager to show me these things? What was she trying to tell me? That these images harboured a deeper truth than the *Priscian*? A singleness, a containment, a sovereignty that could not be proven. A *thereness* free from voices hailing from elsewhere, untrammelled by the quest for lost absolutes? Something about it troubled me, though I still couldn't say exactly what it was.

Inside the low-ceilinged oratory, Raphaëlle showed me the twenty-two tableaux of the Life of Gallus. *Casus Sancti*

Galli. With deft, deliberate movements, she directed me from one to the next. Gallus, the boy prodigy, being presented to Columbanus in Ireland. Arriving with Columbanus in the Valley of Lake Constance. Meeting King Sigisbert and banishing beastly idols to the black lake. Tending the trees of the forest with the help of a tamed bear. Casting demons from the beautiful Fridiburga, daughter of the Duke. Then receiving Fridiburga into monastic life as she kneels before his black-robed body, abandoning her betrothed for this 'higher suitor'. And after that, after the Gallus–Fridiburga exchange? A gap. Pure space!

Why? I asked.

Because, Raphaëlle suggested, the break between Gallus and Columbanus which occurred at that point in the *Life* was a puzzle. All that was known from the various accounts by Walahfried Strabo and Ekkehart IV, cited under the portraits, was that Columbanus left in a hurry, going on to found another monastic settlement in Bobbio and forbidding Gallus to resume further sacerdotal duties until he, Columbanus, was dead. But nobody knows what caused the rift between them, Raphaëlle explained, pushing her camera case back over her shoulder with a twist of her body. It was anybody's guess.

'And your guess?' I asked.

'I don't know,' she said. 'Perhaps the place of the missing picture tells us something.'

'The *place*?'

'Yes. Between the Fridiburga scene and the fall of Gallus.'

'That doesn't tell us *why* Gallus and Columbanus split, does it?'

'It might,' she replied. And, pointing to the picture above our heads with her sleeveless arm, she continued. 'Look again at the picture of Fridiburga kneeling before Gallus! Look at how she's half bent, half rising from her knees; see how she takes that black cloak from Gallus's outstretched hands, her eyes raised towards him. And look at the scarlet-purple colour of Fridiburga's dress – vivid life-blood against Gallus's grizzly robe. Her bare shoulders and neck gleaming white in the sunlight swimming in from the scene behind her – there, you see, where her betrothed, Prince Sigisbert, looks on with a broken heart, outdone on his wedding day by a celibate rival.'

'I still don't see why that should cause a break between master and disciple,' I said, a hint of defensiveness now in my voice.

'Look more closely, then,' Raphaëlle insisted. 'This image may tell us things the official *Life of Gallus* never tells. You see just there how Fridiburga is dressed in purple, not yet black? Do you understand? She is still a Bride of Flesh, not of God. You see? The tension between purple and black makes our eye desert Gallus for the radiant Fridiburga with her ravishing maids, sorrowing prince and wide-eyed children in attendance. Is this the legendary subjection of Fridiburga to Gallus, as the *Life* claims? Surely not! If anything, it is Gallus falling for Fridiburga! That's what the *image* shows, even if the caption says otherwise.'

'You really think that's why Columbanus broke with Gallus?'

'It's maybe not that simple,' Raphaëlle replied. 'But think about it. All the pictures of the *Life of Gallus* up to this have Columbanus at the centre. Suddenly he disappears from the scene, never to reappear. Why? Just think. For years Columbanus mentored the young Gallus, travelled through Britain and Gaul converting tribes and founding settlements – and now, all at once, he beholds a purple-clad lady with bare arms kneeling before his chosen disciple with upturned eyes and open hands. Well? What do you think he feels?'

I didn't reply.

'He feels *jealous*, of course. Don't you see? Just look at the picture again, carefully. Who is the person *not* in the picture? Who is the person *no longer* at the centre? Who is the person you have seen in the other pictures but you do *not* see here?'

'Columbanus,' I replied.

'Exactly,' she exclaimed. 'And the reason you don't see him is because he – like any spectator – is looking at the scene, displaced by Fridiburga from the event itself, cut out of the picture after all those years. He's been cast aside, don't you see, in spite of Gallus's vow never to lower his eyes from heaven, never to lose faith until they both reached the end of the road, the road where all roads lead, symbol of the unifying Word – Rome.'

'Are you saying Columbanus left Gallus behind because Gallus betrayed him?' I inquired finally, more hurt than baffled now.

'No, not because he betrayed him – because Columbanus *believed* he betrayed him. It was all in the mind. A puritan fantasy. But that's how Columbanus saw it at the time; and that's what the painter of this picture saw him seeing. It isn't *said*. It isn't *written*. You probably won't find mention of it in all the documented accounts of the *Casus*. It's unspoken. Unspeakable. But this image *shows* it. Like the sibyls, such things can be banished to the margins, left outside the walls, removed from official stories, left unsaid, but they still find ways to remind us. They still leave traces showing what cannot be said.'

So that was it, I thought to myself as we walked from the Gallus Chapel. That was it, was it? Columbanus betrayed! Gallus fallen! But worse, if these strange things had never happened, St Gallen might never have existed. Its scriptorium might never have been built. The quest for perfection never recorded in its scripts. No jealousy, no fall. No fall, no ascent. Was that the message? I couldn't be sure.

All I knew was that Raphaëlle was still trying to show me something. Signs, warnings, signals about my calling. But she, too, was becoming a riddle to me now. Almost as great as the *Priscian* itself. In a way, I had to admit, I was relieved that she and Jack were leaving for Geneva next day.

'Be wary, for I am indeed a jealous god,' a voice whispered in my head as I followed Raphaëlle out of the chapel.

Entry 26 v

After lunch the next day, Jack and Raphaëlle left for Geneva. But just before they went, Raphaëlle informed me excitedly that she'd made a further discovery, something that proved her hunch. She'd spotted a certain painting of Tobit on the ceiling of the basilica. The blind Tobit, father of Tobias! I hesitated but she was adamant I see it. So, leading me to a spot between the three naves of the Basilica just beneath the central cupola, she gestured upwards to the curvilinear dome. 'You see,' she said, 'there are sixty saints painted up there, but the ones that matter are the two blind ones – Gallus just above us here on this edge of the cupola and Tobit directly opposite.' And sure enough, following the direction of her finger to the top of that blazing roof, I saw them, high above me, just where she'd said: two eyeless holy ones perched like guardian angels around the Holy Trinity. Gallus and Tobit.

But what was Raphaëlle getting at with all this talk of blindness? Images and words? Sightlessness and sight? I knew I should challenge her there, staring into that giant coloured retina as if she were inside the eye of God. I knew that this was the time to nail these giddy conjectures once and for all. But I didn't No. It could wait, I said to myself. Just then I didn't want to speak, to interrogate, to counter, only to stand there behind Raphaëlle, her hair pulled up over brown shoulders, in the quiet evening hush of that huge basilica, gazing into its efflorescent dome.

On our way back to join the others, Raphaëlle touched me lightly on the arm outside the basilica doors and said: 'Stop listening to other voices, Sam. Follow your own. Open your eyes and see what's around you. You've been looking too hard. It's everywhere.'

She left with Jack that afternoon.

Anselm and I stayed on in St Gallen for the rest of the week, making the most of Klaus's expert knowledge and the actual presence of the Index. Indeed, so impressed was Klaus that, at the end of our visit, he gave permission for us to bring the Index back to Columbanus Abbey, on temporary loan, for the few weeks necessary to complete the revised edition. Anselm had always been like a brother to him, he said, ever since his novitiate days. He knew he would guard it with his life. Besides, if anyone could get to the bottom of all this, Klaus wagered with his impish smile, it was Anselm and I.

Entry 27
Columbanus Abbey, 6 August 1977

Feast of the Transfiguration

The night of my return from St Gallen I couldn't sleep. Lying on my bed, staring at the blank ceiling, I had a waking dream. Again and again I turned the reverie over in my mind, weaving and unweaving, toying and threading at will, until the scenes knit themselves into a burning, graphic whole.

I am in the scriptorium archive in St Gallen, sitting at a desk by a row of bookshelves. The *Priscian* Index lies open in front of me, a copy of Arno Borst's *Der Turmbau von Babel* beside it. The smell of beeswax mixes with the musty scent of old hide bindings. A small lamp shines in a corner, giving off an odd grey light, a light of many greys – pewter, ashen, silver, copper-grey. I hear the voice of a woman, humming softly to herself, muffled at first but then growing clearer, distinct. The words of a song: '*Il était un petit navire . . .*' It is Raphaëlle.

She moves across the room and sits up on the desk in front of me, raising a hand to lift stray curls of hair escaping from the chignon at the nape of her neck. Her skin glistens in the grey air as I reach my hands towards her. She looks at me as I touch her, her forehead puckering at intervals, eyes opening and closing as if stinging from salt, some inner light swimming up from the deep of her brown-green irises, loosened by the disturbance of a long-buried secret. The two of us there, one kneeling, one upright, like Gallus and Fridiburga – but in reverse, she above, I below.

I bury my head between her outspread legs as she reclines above me, arms stretched behind on to the wide desk strewn with papers and pens. Raphaëlle stays like that, immobile, mute, impassive, as my hands part her shirt, my mouth burrowing deeper and deeper between her raised knees and scooped velvet thighs. I am like a desert hermit, crazed by some forbidden scent, thirsting for a deep-sunk well.

Only once does Raphaëlle move, lifting a hand to push her hair back. The arc of her rising arm grazes an inkwell on the desk behind us, splashing a shower of bright blue fluid. The ink spreads from the centre of the Index parchment to its curling serrated edges. Then, urging me to my feet with an ink-stained hand, and adjusting her clothes with the other, she gazes straight at me, her features lustrous now, sibylline, illuminated from the inside. We leave the scriptorium together.

THE LIFE OF TOBIAS

PART SIX

'Let us run after Thee towards the odour of Thy perfumes, and, let My soul cling unto Thee; that with these songs we may speedily pass through the world, for unless we long unweariedly with heavenly desires, we needs must be entangled in earthly ones. Let us as pilgrims ever desire our homeland; for the end of the road is ever the object of travellers' desires, entangled by no lusts, longing with no earthly desires . . . My soul thirsts for the mighty and living God, like a waterless land before thee, I desire to be dissolved.

The Works of St Columbanus, Instructio VIII, 1–2. AD 612

∫

Entry 28
Columbanus Abbey, 20 August, 1977

Feast of St Bernard of Clairvaux

Entry 28 i

I gave Anselm a copy of my St Gallen fantasy, just as I'd entered it here in my journal. Nothing withheld from my Abbot and Confessor. He read it but didn't really say much at the time, apart from recalling Columbanus's rule about discerning correctly in doubtful cases. Not another word about it then for two weeks until he called me to his room last evening.

He showed me a chair as I entered, fixing a smile somewhere between intimacy and distance.

'I think you are ready now,' he said to me.

'For what?' I asked, taking my seat.

'For your final work.'

'But I haven't finished with the Index yet. I need more time,' I protested.

'I'm not talking about that, Tobias,' he said, raising a hand. 'I'm talking about the real work, the one that really matters. You understand, don't you?'

'I don't think so.' I swallowed, sitting back in my chair.

'Even after your fantasy – betraying Jack, me, God – you say you still don't understand?'

'No.'

'I am talking about the essence of Columbanus's Rule. What I have been trying to teach you since you entered the novitiate. That to be raised you must first be lowered, into the abyss, into the emptiness, into the very darkness of yourself, the nothingness. What Columbanus called *mortificatio*.'

'Is that why the Scriptures say that God's power thrives in weakness?' I ventured calmly, my tone softening to match his.

Anselm made an acquiescent gesture, then continued. 'Yes. But there's a harder side to it, more unspeakable. It's not just a question of meekness inheriting kingdoms.' He opened his hands. 'It's a question of light coming from darkness, grace from disgrace, good from evil. Remember Luke 2: "He is set for the fall and the rising of many . . . and your own soul a sword shall pierce". Recall the patterns of Revelation. Adam's fall, Job's terror, Isaac's blindness, Joseph's bondage, Daniel's den, Jonah's whale, Isaiah's cave.' He paused suddenly, leaning over his desk. 'Even Gallus had to fall and lose his eyes before the greatest scriptorium of Christendom could come into existence.'

'But if God's Word is already revealed in Scripture,' I asked, 'why are we still looking for the secret?'

'Because so few have ears to hear. Even when the Word stripped itself and exposed itself to nakedness – Christ incarnate, Christ abandoned, Christ crucified – even then only a handful heeded the call. God went that far. Just think of it, Tobias. To the *unum purum nihil* of utter extinction. Penetration of the hands, the feet, the side, the total being. Prostration and purgation without limit. Beyond good and evil. Absolute self-emptying, reckless courage. Mad love. Kenosis.' Anselm's face gleamed.

'Was that his descent into hell?'

'His descent into the darkness of the damned, where he fetched terrible imaginings from our basest depths and brought them back to the radiance of God. "Like Jonah's three nights in the belly of the sea-monster, for three nights the Son of Man descends into the belly of the earth".'

He stopped then, abruptly, and looked away from me, out of the window (it was already dark outside), as though he wanted to distract himself, slow things down, retrieve his calm.

I hesitated. He let the silence lengthen. At last I blurted out: 'What are you really saying, Anselm?'

'I am saying you must follow the same pattern, go down into the darkness, empty your desire into the nothing . . .'

'What desire?'

'The desire recorded in your journal.'

'But that's just *fantasy*. Not something I really want.'

Anselm shook his head. His voice was solemn. 'It is what part of you wants – the part of you that God wants back. And it is because you've finally owned that part that you can now disown it . . .'

I felt a sudden thrill – whether of fear or ecstasy, I wasn't sure.

'You are ready,' he went on, 'to surrender your desire: and that is how your desire will be redeemed – by God, your God and mine, who is pleased with your sacrifice, who placed us on this earth with the evil *yezer* and dared to say on the Seventh Day of Creation that it was "good". Once you surrender your desire to Him. He will replace it with his own.'

I said nothing. Just waited there, attentive, for Anselm to continue. 'God *needs* us, Tobias, God needs *us* more than we need *Him*. Without us He is alone with His desire –

unrequited, thirsting, desperate. You know what it is like, Tobias, don't you? You've felt it too.'

'Then what must I do?' I whispered.

'Nothing. Trust God, that is all. And He will empty you. To the pit of your being, until there is nothing left of you, nothing but essence – pure essence, His essence.'

I trusted. I followed Anselm from his room in the cloister across the quad to the Chapel. Everything was lit up inside, a pure spectral whiteness of walls, pillars, side aisles and classic Roman archways – the space between man and God. But we were going to a deeper space, beneath man and God, beneath good and evil, under the earth. Anselm opened the heavy wooden door behind the choir stall and we descended the steps into the chamber. It was totally dark until Anselm lit the candles. Then it flickered into visibility, bit by bit, the central vault in the shape of a cross with the semi-circular altar at the far end. The ninth-century iron cross by the right nave and the twelfth-century wooden one by the left. Then the three large icons – Christ the Healer, Madonna of Zagorsk, Angel of St Gallen – suspended from the ceiling in cast-iron tubular frames with tiny silver lamps at the base. There was a smell of burnt wax and stale incense (the previous Sunday the Abbey choir had packed the cramped space to perform a two-hour liturgy of Slavonic polyphony).

Anselm said hardly anything. He was in perfect control, sure of every move, as if performing a prepared rite. He led me before the altar, had me take off my shoes, then lie down flat on the earthen floor. The cold flagstones steadied my stomach and legs, and I could feel against my skin the rough outlines of animal shapes, cast from old iron utensils hammered into the floor in twisted frames. *Mortal, this is the place for the soles of my feet, where I will reside among the people of Israel forever.* Anti-icons of underworld energy. I had never before realized why they were there, why the

Abbot declined to remove them when this basement was renovated to house the icons. Now I knew. The *struggle*. In this underground place the struggle raged. Yes, I knew it now with every sinew of my being as I lifted my eyes to behold the black square etched into the marble altar in front of me – first face, last face, good face, evil face, empty face. Zero of form. Pure space.

'Are you ready?' I heard Anselm say equably from somewhere above me.

'Yes,' I said.

'Do you desire?'

'Yes.'

'Do you renounce desire?'

'Yes.'

'Are you ready to do God's will?'

'Yes.'

'Whatever His will may be?'

'Yes.'

'Without question?'

'Yes.'

'To the end?'

'Yes.'

'Into the basest darkness?'

'Yes.'

'Into the nothing?'

'Yes.'

Silence then. For what seemed like hours. I didn't count. My mind was empty, incapable of counting or thinking or praying. I felt nothing after a while, not even the cold flagstones, not even the sharp edges of the iron shapes beneath me. Nothing. I must have slipped into sleep, unconsciousness, oblivion, *Unum purum nihil*.

Then it came. The terrible searing flame. From the base of my feet to the tip of my head. A monstrous tearing inside me. As though I was being ripped apart, broken into bits, sundered and splintered and emptied out into nowhere.

Falling deeper and deeper, far beneath the skies, beneath the earth, into a dark bottomless sea. *Abyssus abyssum invocat.* And as I drifted lower and lower, the burning inside me eased and I opened my eyes, and saw frantic creatures writhing about me, in a blur of desperate motion, creatures of the depths with gaping mouths, compact of slime, convulsed by spasms of unspeakable pain. Scavengers taking monstrous pleasure with soft-skinned corpses. Porpeagles, makoes, thrashers, orcs. Scurrying black morsels of snout, eyes, teeth, gills. White bellies. Black tails. Then deeper again until I was surrounded by scaled creatures with silver-green eyes, splayed tongues and webbed limbs. Cleft-footed sibyls of the fathomless sea. Then blackness again. Pure emptiness.

And I opened my ears. And I heard a voice saying, 'Come back. Sam, come back.'

And other signals – from farther away. Prague, Ankara, Lahti, Paris, Lille, Stockh'm, Hilversum, Rome.

Then a final voice, answering, saying, 'Write down what you have seen, Tobias, things that happened and things to come ... the vision you have seen by the River Chebar, the sound like the sound of mighty waters ... I kill and I make alive, Tobias, I wound and I heal when I whet my flashing sword ...'

Entry 28 ii

I take my final vows in September. My notes for the revised *Priscian* are now virtually complete (summarized in appendix form below). Working closely with Anselm I should be finished before Advent. Unlike Cilian, unlike Jack, I have observed the calling. It is from God, and it is mine.

As to what I have recorded here in the twenty-eight entries in this journal, I do not know if it has any worth. But I have done everything to follow Columbanus's Rule, to 'complete the tale of the work, believing what the superior commands is right'. Now that I have climbed the ladder, up and down, I push it from me. It has served its purpose. The only thing I add are the words of a twelfth-century Irish scribe who, terminating some ancient codex I saw copied in St Gallen, wrote: 'I, who have written this history, or rather fable, am doubtful about many things in it. For some of them are the figments of demons, some of them poetic imaginings, some true, some not, some for the delight of fools.'

Post-Scriptum
Myrtleville, 29 August 1977, 1 a.m.

Memorial, John the Baptist

I thought it was over. Once and for all. But I was wrong.

Why did I invite her here tonight? After what happened with Anselm in the Icon Chamber, I was so certain I'd won the struggle. But it wasn't enough for *me* to be certain – I had to make Raphaëlle certain too. I had to prove it to her. Just one hour. Here in Myrtleville. Tonight. That's all it would take, I'd said to her in my note. It was urgent.

I was wrong.

She arrived down from Cork forty minutes late, awkward as a stranger, but self-possessed as ever. She'd left Jack reading in the flat, she explained. He knew nothing. She couldn't stay long. Pulling back her tossed hair, she kept remarking how warm it was here in the chalet, sheltered from the gale gusting in from the sea. She poured herself a glass of water and we stood at opposite ends of the wide bay window. Raphaëlle gazed into the night towards the sea, although it was already dark – 11 p.m.

I told her what had happened in the Icon Chamber, every detail. Diving under the water, down into the belly of the whale, swallowed by blackness, then rising suddenly to light, to new life in God. I told her Anselm had been right all along. Right about my calling, my wrestling with angels, my work on the *Priscian*. I was ready now for final vows. I admitted she had been the other voice in me all this time, ever since I'd first met her here in Myrtleville: the voice that had to be finally answered, silenced, before I took the last step.

As I spoke, Raphaëlle kept looking out of the window, gazing towards the sea she couldn't see, intermittently swirling the water in her glass, as if in rhythm with the beating of waves below on the rocks.

When I'd finished speaking, she looked at me and said: 'Sam, you listen to too many voices. Why don't you listen to your own?' As she uttered those words, she arched an arm up over her head, lifting her hair up at the back. And, slowly, I found my hand reaching towards her until it touched the bared nape of her neck and rose upwards to where her hair lifted in a crest. Brush of a wave. Soft bark of Lebanese cedar. Shudder of a boat's keel on the skin of a whale.

One touch and I knew she was right not to believe me. One touch and I *was* my desire. Nothing but desire. All hers.

That was an hour ago. Now she's gone, back to Cork. To Jack. It is done and it is over. I know nothing more. I hear the gale blowing in from the sea. Black waters beating off the rocks below in Poul Gorm. I close my eyes, tight, tight, but all I see is the great curling waves, hollow in the centre, breaking into arms of foam.

∫

AFTERWORD

Jack closes the journal and sits back in the chair, his face in
his hands. Why did it happen? Why did Sam drown? Falling
into the sea at Poul Gorm that morning. Still clutching a
camera in his hand when they discovered the body. Did
he die by accident, swept away by a freak wave? Or was
it by design? What did Sam mean when he wrote that 'it
was over'? What happened between him and Raphaëlle?

Jack wishes he'd never read the journal. He remains
seated at Sam's desk for several minutes, staring at the
faded picture on the cover – the drawing of the horse
staring back at him, familiar now, all too familiar. Roddy
Owen. Cheltenham champion. Another stolen fantasy. He
takes a silver paper-knife from Sam's desk and removes the
Sellotape rim around the cut-out. He folds the drawing
in two and puts it in his pocket, almost without looking,
without thinking, his eyes vacant. He replaces the dappled
volume on Sam's shelf where he had found it between the
Priscian files.

Twenty past two, Sam's bedside clock says. Jack has been
reading for almost three hours. Yet he isn't tired. Numb,
yes, but not tired. He sits down on Sam's bed and gazes

across at the replica of the icon, then at the mirror beside him. He is as wide-eyed as the Angel. He lies back on Sam's bed, one arm over his face, the other thrown behind his head. He stays like that for what seems like ages, but is only a moment. Then he rises from the bed and strides out.

He pads through the dark corridors like a sleepwalker, one hand in his pocket clutching the counterfeit copy of Roddy Owen, the pencil-traced, coloured-in horse.

'It is done and it is over. It is done and it is over.' Jack repeats Sam's words in his mind. What was going on between him and Raphaëlle all that time? He had noticed nothing. Not this time nor the other times Sam wrote of in his journal: the times Raphaëlle questioned his calling, going on with all her stories of sybils and prophetesses and the missing picture of Gallus?

Jack turns into the corridor leading to the cloistered quad. His face is drawn, as he staggers under another lash of doubt. How deep did the betrayal go? Was Raphaëlle taken by Sam from the start, from the time she'd first met him in Myrtleville three years ago, teasing him with endless questions and confiding intimate memories? Did she really lead Sam on? Or was Sam the seducer? All that tormented lust he wrote of in his journal. Was it just fantasy? Or did he finally act it out? When he reached the guest room, Jack would wake Raphaëlle and ask her all these things.

His steps agitated now, Jack passes through the open quad separating the monastic building from the school. For a moment shadows from the rhododendron bushes outside the archway make eddies of moonlight against the granite cloister walls like children playing with water. There is a noise – the squeak of a bat or a hinge twisting in the light breeze. He steps into the school entrance hall and heads directly to the sleeping quarters. Reaching the guest dorm, he swings open the door and switches on the light.

Raphaëlle's bed is empty, her bedclothes thrown back like a tossed wave. Standing at the doorway, Jack scrutinizes the mound of pillows and blankets. Then he moves on to check the adjoining dormitories, one after another. His pace grows fitful as he strides back down the long flagstoned alley, with its line of latticed lockers, to the entrance hall. He puts his hand to his neck; it's wet. He shivers. Where is she?

Raphaëlle rises abruptly from the chair on the far side of the Abbot's large oak desk, scattering papers. She turns her back to Anselm, strides to the window, concealing the flush of confusion that darkens her face and throat. She had come to look for Jack but now finds herself seized by the Abbot's inquisitive stare.

'Why did Sam die?' Anselm asks.

'Maybe he couldn't live with his desire . . .' Raphaëlle collects herself. Her words come slowly as if she is just discovering them. 'I don't believe Sam really knew what he wanted. He lived his life by halves, he was always standing in for someone, missing something, listening for some voice, filling some gap left empty for him.'

The Abbot's hands grasp the desk in front of him; the knuckles are white. 'And his calling? What about his calling?'

But Raphaëlle carries on as though she doesn't hear him. 'I felt if I could reach him, get through to that *missing* part . . .'

'. . . that *missing* part belonged to God,' Anselm interrupts. His eyes blaze.

'To God? Or to you, Anselm?' Raphaëlle's words slice through the air. 'Can you not see how dangerous it is to play at God?' She faces Anselm squarely, his profile stark against the stippled window. But the Abbot's fierce gaze cannot silence her now. 'You manipulated Sam. You taught him that desire is death, the last obstacle, the ultimate sacrifice. And he believed you.'

Jack paces along the empty linoleumed corridor of the school extension with its faint scent of floor polish and schoolboy sweat left over from the summer term. He passes the senior classroom with its rows of bare wooden desks oddly luminous in the first glimmer of dawn, and thinks of Cilian towering by the blackboard all those years ago, a book held high in his hand as he declaimed to captive charges. And he thinks of Sam – who would have been teaching in this very room next term. Sam. His brother. 'It is done and it is over'. Why did he do it? Why did he drown? Will Raphaëlle have the answers?

He scours the entire school building, but there's still no sign of her. He is exhausted now; a little pulse throbs in the corner of one eye; sweat trickles down his back. He needs air, a walk, through the grounds. Maybe that's where Raphaëlle has gone. Yes, he will search for her in the grounds.

The early morning air cools him for a moment. The high oaks and redwoods beyond the east garden shimmer in the pale light. *Sequoia sempervirens, Sequoiadendron giganteum*, Jack finds himself murmuring, half consciously. The trees that Anselm named but never touched – no, never touched – each time he led them on this walk as schoolboys. He remembers too the shuffling sound of the Abbot's long habit, echoing the flurry of dry leaves whispering among themselves. And the unforgotten lines from Hosea he invariably cited as they walked – 'He shall strike root like the forests of Lebanon./ He shall again live beneath my shadow./ He shall flourish as a garden . . . /O Ephraim, what have I to do with idols?'

The belly of a cloud glows reddish above the tips of eucalyptus circling the Black Lake. Jack crosses the small stone bridge over the nearby stream and notices the enormous lysichitum lilies spread lazily across the water. He imagines himself striding behind Anselm, passing the dignified Himalayan rhododendrons and sleek Scots pines draped in dew from the moist August night. He hasn't forgotten the name of a single species. They seem to name themselves, in his head, in Anselm's voice. Douglas firs. Sitka spruces. Sierra redwoods. Ilchester oaks. The silent monologue of the soul murmurs on inside him, sounds eliding in such intimacy that he can no longer tell if the inner voice is the Abbot's or his own or Sam's. It is as though he is at one again with his past, with the self he left behind when he left the Abbey, the self that followed behind Abbot Anselm through this landscape of leaf and bark. Jack closes his eyes, still imagining he's tracing Anselm's steps, stray odours of tree fungus and rotting wood the only sentient reminders of change. When he opens his eyes again, the grey of early morning is already yielding to a slow efflorescence of pale browns, yellows and greens. A crescent sun curves over the horizon beyond the trees, like a stranded whale, irradiating a halo of bilious light. He has described a circle, Jack realizes, as he walks from the oak wood at the end of the avenue along the gravelled road back to the Abbey.

For a while he'd forgotten he was looking for Raphaëlle. As he remembers, his face fills with urgency. He comes to a stop directly opposite the cluster of cedars and pines. But he does not name them this time, as Anselm had always named them, neither out loud nor to himself. No. He moves towards them now and touches them, one after another. He reaches the tall Lebanese cedar in the middle of the cluster, the old trysting place, and draws his hand along the bark. The wood is blistered and seasoned from years of inclement weather. Its harsh, chipped surface takes him aback (he had remembered it as being much smoother). Anger rises steadily inside him like a burning resin. He thinks of Raphaëlle, then of Anselm, but both images rapidly fade. Only one face remains. Sam's. And it will not go away. Jack lowers his head and lets his hand descend the bark blindly until he comes upon a blunt strip of root lying loose at the base of the trunk. He grips it fiercely in both hands, like Esau's rod, and suddenly feels rage. Tighter and tighter he grips it now, his rod and his staff, as lines come rushing into his head. When I whet my flashing sword I will take vengeance on my adversary . . . Strike root in the forests of Lebanon . . . Strike root in the forests . . . Strike root . . . Strike!

He hurries back to the Abbey, the stem of wood still clutched firmly in his hand.

'You seem to blame me for Sam's death.' Anselm plaits both hands in a concentrated pose; the gesture restores him. 'Yet you, Raphaëlle, were the last to see him alive. You were the one to seduce him, to take away his calling.'

'You understand nothing, Anselm.'

Anselm's mouth tightens, then relaxes. 'I read the final entry in Sam's journal.'

'Sam wrote something before he died?'

'Yes.'

'After I left him at Myrtleville?'

The Abbot nods a second time.

'What did he say?'

'"It is done and it is over." That's what he said.'

Raphaëlle's shoulders drop. She tries to look past Anselm at the morning light spilling in through the window, but all she sees is the taut outline of his frame rising from the desk.

She meets his stare, as he asks, 'What will Jack think?'

'Jack?' Raphaëlle echoes. 'Jack knows nothing . . .'

'He too has read Sam's journal. In Sam's room. Tonight.'

There is alarm in Raphaëlle's face. 'How?'

Anselm looms over his desk, but his tone softens. 'The journal was with Sam's papers. I knew Jack would find his way to it. I checked Sam's room shortly after midnight. I heard Jack inside.'

'You *wanted* Jack to read it!' Raphaëlle draws back. Her fingers spread wide against her forehead. 'You wanted him to enter Sam's secret life, didn't you? To know about that final meeting in Myrtleville.' She hesitates for an awful moment, 'And now that Sam is gone, you want Jack back!'

Anselm stands rigid. He closes his eyes as if concentrating on something in his mind. Then he continues evenly. 'It is God who wants Jack back. Not I.'

Raphaëlle bridles. 'You can't. You can't do with Jack what you did with Sam.'

Anselm looks away.

'You knew all along about Sam's obsession, didn't you?' Raphaëlle persists. 'You fed his fantasies all this time, leading him on to see me as some alluring Eve. You were preparing him all these years. Preparing him to yield up his desire. I was just a pawn in the plan, wasn't I? You were the real seducer, Anselm, not me!'

Anselm's features flare with anger, but he holds back. In a low voice, he eventually responds: 'What I did, I did for God. Things happen at times, not as one wills or plans them, but according to some higher, inscrutable, design. Some of us are called to read those signs. And some of us respond. That is something you can never understand, Raphaëlle. But Sam understood it. And now that he's read the journal, I believe that Jack will understand it too.'

Raphaëlle slowly shakes her head from side to side; her voice drops, her body trembles, but her eyes do not waver. 'I'm leaving here. I'm going back to Geneva, and Jack is coming with me.'

'Jack will need time,' Anselm answers. 'Now that he's read the journal he'll need to stay on here for a while, to clear his head, to pray.'

'He'll come,' Raphaëlle says. 'I know he will.'

'God will decide.'

The Abbot's features are composed again now, as imperturbable as before. But he winces as the door to the room swings open. Jack enters, wielding the cedar root.

He looks first at Raphaëlle, who takes a step towards him; then at Anselm, who straightens, recoiling slightly.

'It's unspeakable!' Jack spits out each syllable 'Unspeakable!'

The words are addressed to no one in particular, to a space somewhere between Raphaëlle and Anselm, both standing motionless now on either side of the desk. Then, after a pause, Jack raises the stick slowly into the air with both hands. It hangs suspended, like the blade of an executioner, waiting to fall. For several seconds he holds it there, glancing now at Raphaëlle, now at Anselm. Then he lowers it gradually, towards the floor.

'Strike root! Strike!' Jack mumbles in a flurry of half-articulate cries. 'Strike! Sam! Tobias! Drowned! Got away! Again! Gone!'

He falls silent, inclines his head with a stifled sob and sinks into the large carved space of the Abbot's empty chair.

One week later, Jack is able to leave the infirmary and make a visit to the church.

It is dark and empty inside as Jack enters, the smell of stale candlewax and incense recalling Sam's funeral. He moves up the centre aisle, towards the vacant stalls where Anselm and the monks had stood and mourned, Brothers in Christ. He walks straight towards the altar, just as he had that day, but no coffin rests upon his shoulder now. No dead brother to carry to the Father Abbot. And no Raphaëlle to weep.

He does not stop at the altar, though. He continues past it until he comes to the entrance to the Icon Chamber at the back of the church. It is open. He descends the narrow steps and stands in the stone-panelled space in front of the gold iconostasis. He switches on the wall lamps illuminating the icon of St Gallen from both sides. Approaching it slowly, he stares at the image of the Angel. How often he had gazed upon this face. In daytime reverie or nighttime sleep, the enormous melting, dark-ringed eyes had haunted him. Eyes that stared right back at him, as they do now. The sensual mouth, the scooped cheeks, the pale-crested, in-folded wings. The image had never left him, not since he and Sam first beheld it all those years ago on their arrival at the Abbey.

'Help me,' Jack says to the icon. 'Help me discern the voices. Help me know which is which.' He shuts his eyes and, after a while, begins to hear a rustling noise inside his head. Leaves. Robes. Voices. A low voice at first, calm, even-toned, far-off but drawing close. The Abbot's voice. Anselm:

It is a sign. The sign Tobias sought. Revealed at last. The Priscian *Index. The hidden code. It has come through. The night Sam drowned. Ink spilt on the page. By accident? By design? What does it matter? The ink seeped through the parchment until the letters began to show, tiny secret letters peering out from within the page. Minuscule tails and tressed heads worming their way into vision. A frieze of scribblings scarcely visible beneath the blackened surface, furling and unfurling in little grey curves, tendrils and curlicues shining brighter and brighter, until they gradually lined up into words, rows, sentences, verses. A palimpsest – text behind text, script behind script. The oldest game in the oldest book, and somehow it escaped us all. But Sam's fall, his death, has made it visible at last. Sam did not die for nothing. The letters are there now, all linked together at last to reveal the code. The secret of Gairthigern. The secret of Gallus's fall.* Casus Sancti Galli. *Now your call is clear, Jack. Take Sam's place and finish the work. Read the signs, decipher the Logos, discern the message of God's long-lost tongue. Strike root like the forests of Lebanon. Remember the Rule of Columbanus: 'Ask Thy Father and He will show you'. Take your place again, Jack, your original place, the place of Brother Tobias.*

Anselm's voice grows muffled and fades. There is silence for a moment, then more whispering. Other voices. Jack strains to listen. Strange tongues, long-distance, one after another, each drowning out the other, each becoming nearer, more familiar than the other. *Ankara, Lahti, Paris, Prague, Nice, Stockh'm, Rome, West, Welsh, Berlin, Strasbourg, Hilversum, Brussels, Athlone, Luxembourg, Light, Hamburg, Scottish, Lisbon, Sundsvall, Munich, Geneva.*

Geneva. Jack can hear more clearly now. A voice calling inside him from somewhere beyond him, from the future perhaps, whether distant or near he cannot tell. Compelling. Singular. Unmistakable now. The voice of Raphaëlle.

I am back in my element, Jack. Head to water. I am swimming in Lake Geneva. Arms stretched full and palms wide open, I glide through the waves. If I open my eyes now I see nothing, only dark, only black. I do not open them. Not because I am afraid – no, I have no fear – but because I have no need to see what is beneath me. I know the water is bottomless.

Far from shore now, I see you, Jack. What do you see? What are you looking at? The eyes of the Angel of St Gallen? The eyes of Anselm? Sam's eyes? What did Sam see, in that final moment when he fell from the rocks into the sea? Did he stare down into the fathomless pool?

If it is over, it is over. Il ne faut rien regretter. My head turns in and out of the smooth black water, my open mouth blowing down into the silvery dark, then rising up again to suck air back into my body. The waves hold and caress me here as I move buoyant over their surface. Liquid, cool flames. They know, these waves; I have no fear. My arms are beating down now, stroke after stroke, and I do not need to think any more. Thoughts disappear. Then words. Only images remain. Can you see them too? Will you come to me, Jack? Will you? Deep calling upon deep in a roar of waters. Living waters. Yes. Living. Swimming for life. To the far shore.

The following appendices were found in a batch of loose sheets at the end of Sam's journal after his death. The first includes the Notes he was researching for the Priscian edition (1974–1977), liberal interpretations of the ancient texts, together with a number of miscellaneous visuals related to the project. The second contains a selection of the Night Fragments which he and Anselm worked on during the winter of 1975–1976. The third was added by Anselm himself shortly after Sam's death.

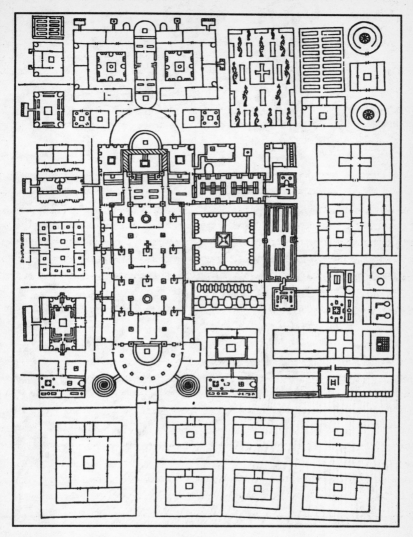

Plan of the monastery of St. Gall, about 820. Copy of the Carolingian parchment document in the Library of St. Gall (redrawn to facilitate reading): Double-choir with numerous altars and a pair of round towers; right, adjoining cloister with cloister-walk; above novitiate and cemetery; left, abbot's house, school, guesthouse and sanitorium; below and on the right, agricultural buildings.

Detail of a woodcut of the town of St. Gallen by Heinrich Vogtherr.

VERBUM DOMINI MANET INTERNUM

(From the Department of Prints and Drawings of the Zentralbibliothek, Zurich)

Map tracing some of the stopping points on the main part of the route travelled by Columbanus and Gallus in the early 7th century from Bangor to St. Gallen.

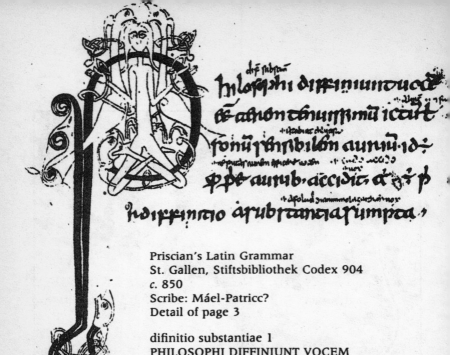

Priscian's Latin Grammar
St. Gallen, Stiftsbibliothek Codex 904
c. 850
Scribe: Máel-Patricc?
Detail of page 3

difinitio substantiae 1
PHILOSOPHI DIFFINIUNT VOCEM

ESSE AEREM TENUISSIMUM ICTUM VEL
.i. citabiat chlúasa 2
SONUM SENSIBILEM AURIUM ID EST
.i. ne putas aurem efficere vocem 3 .i. cado, accido 4 .i. vox 5
QUOD PROPRIE AURIBUS ACCIDIT, ET EST PRIOR
.i. afolad dianimmolngaithær vox 6
DIFFINITIO A SUBSTANTIA SUMPTA

Philosophers define voice as very fine air which has been struck or as
a sound which is apparent to the ears, that is to say which especially
strikes the ears and the first definition is taken from its substance . . .

Glosses:
1 the definition of substance [Latin]
2 i.e. which ears perceive [Old Irish]
3 i.e so that you should not think that it is the ear which produced
the voice [Latin]
4 i.e. (cado) I fall (accido) I fall upon [an etymological gloss]
5 i.e. voice [Latin]
6 i.e. the substance from which *vox* is produced [Old Irish]

∫

APPENDIX I

NOTES ON THE *ST GALL PRISCIAN* AND *INDEX*
Brother Tobias Toland

1.1 The *St Gall Priscian* is a grammar consisting of 16 books, copied and glossed by Irish scribes in the 840s and preserved in leather-covered boards in the Irish collection of manuscripts in St Gallen, known as the *Libri Scottici Scripti*. Some volumes may have been taken away by theologians attending the Councils of Constance and Basle in the fifteenth century or destroyed in the religious wars of the Reformation. But most have survived and today comprise an edition of some 240 pages.

1.2 A version of the original Latin Grammar composed by the Greek scholar Priscian in Constantinople in AD 500, and entitled *Institutio de Arte Grammatica*, the *St Gall Priscian* has the unique distinction of being annotated in both Latin and Gaelic by Irish scribes engaged in the re-evangelization of pagan Europe. The Grammar was seen by some ninth-century commentators as a blueprint for the establishment of a Universal Language for the Holy Roman Empire transcending the internecine tribal divisions of the Dark Ages.

1.3 The migrant Irish monks who first brought the commented text of the Grammar to St Gallen, the most celebrated scriptorium of its time, were part of a monastic movement know as *Céli Dé* (or 'Vassals of God'). These scholars subscribed to the belief that existing vernaculars were fallen derivations of an original Perfect Tongue, reputed to be the language spoken by Yahweh when he created the world. This original language was known as *Gairthigern* in Old Irish, from the root words *Gair + tigern* meaning 'voice of the Lord'. Some scholars related this to the *Vox Domini* of the Psalter. *Gairthigern* was the name for the single world language destroyed by the Tower of Babel. The term occurs in such diverse texts as the *Lebor Gabála Érenn* and the *Historia Brittonum* and is often related to the origin legend of the Gaelic language. At the Tower of Babel, after the confusion of tongues, a man named Fenius Farsaid formed a language called *Goídelc* or Gaelic made up of the best features of the newly-separated 72 languages. His brother, the eponymous Goidel Mac Aingin, became the first speaker of this synthetic tongue (and was later known as Gael Glas or the 'bright-green Gael'). The Irish scribes of the seventh and eight centuries would have been familiar with these accounts recycled in such learned texts as the *Bretha Nemed, Hisperica Farmina, Collectio Hibernensis* or the widely circulated Gaelic Primer of Poets known as the *Úraiceacht Éicse*.

1.4 Already in the time of Gallus and Columbanus, the quest for a language transcending tribal differences was advanced by the *Céle Dé* movement. This sought a more spiritual and ascetic role for the scriptoriums and repudiated attachments to the native Gaelic chieftains with their pagan tales of genealogy and law (e.g. the Conception of Cúchulainn or the Voyage of Bran). The most decisive turn in this reformist movement came in the early ninth century when the pious Abbot of the Bangor School, in which Columbanus and Gallus had been trained, established a new Abbey in Castledermot which became known as *dísert Diarmada* (Diarmaid's Retreat) on account of its exceptionally ascetic Rule and Penitential. Many of the famous manuscripts of the period were composed there before being transported by migrating monks to the Continent, including the celebrated *Milan Codex*, the *Antiphonary of Bangor* and the *Gall Priscian* itself with its marginal eulogies to 'Sanctus Diormitius'. A distinct line of succession can thus be established from the Bangor school of Columbanus and Gallus in the early seventh century and the great manuscripts of Diarmaid's school in the ninth, so many of which found their way to the eponymous Abbey of Gallus where they are housed to this day in the renowned *Scottici Scripti*.

1.5 Contrary to the Hisperic claim that the monasticism of Gallus and Columbanus originated in a culture of tribal division, and contrary to the legacy of internecine rivalry between native sages (*Immacallamh an dá Túarad*), the *Gall Priscian* represents a text devoted to the pursuit of unity through language. It is no accident that this manuscript is a centrepiece of the learned texts brought from Ireland to heathen Europe between the seventh and ninth centuries. It might even be hailed as the crowning achievement of Gallus and Columbanus who came to save the Continent from the ravages of the Dark Ages, reintroducing the dream of a Unified Logos to transcend the warring tongues and reunite the world once more, after the Fall, after Babel, after the crucifixion of Word-made-Flesh, the Living Lord, Jesus Christ. The *Gall Priscian* was a vital weapon in this search for a Unified Grammar which might retrieve the scattered members of a divided cosmos into new harmony. Along with Hebrew and Greek, a perfected cosmopolitan Latin was to be the third language of the sacred Trinity devoted to the restoration of the Revealed Word.

1.6 The scribe of the *Gall Priscian* is one Máel-Patricc (c. 850). The names of several other Irish scribes are also mentioned in the margins of the text – Coirpre, Ferdomnach, Cobthach, Ruaidrí, Donngus, Finguine, Máel Brigte – giving rise to many erroneous assertions that the script was the work of dual or multiple authorship. In particular there was the suggestion that Máel-Patricc fought with his rival scribe, Coirpre, and ended up dividing the rights of transcription. But it is now almost certain that the occurrence of Coirpre's name, along with the others, is no more than a ruse of pseudonymity deployed by Máel-Patricc to pay homage to his confrères at the scriptorium of Castledermot where the manuscript was composed. The mistaken assumption of hybrid authorship has been compounded, I believe, by equally mistaken hypotheses about the origin of the script. Several commentators and scholars over the years have confused the original Armagh hand with the Iona and Bangor schools, alluding in particular to occasional alternations between thin and thick strokes, between hair-line horizontals and broad verticals. But the recent discovery of the missing *Index*, written in the inimitable hand of the Armagh-trained Máel-Patricc, seems to confirm the claim for a single author. The variations in script-type, I suggest, are more likely due to contingent factors such as: Máel-Patricc cutting his quill to different widths during the composition of the manuscript; alterable qualities of the vellum caused by inconsistent preparation of the page: different uses of pounce; or simply to writer's cramp necessitating rotation of the pen between left and right hands.

1.7 Máel-Patricc and the other scribes at Castledermot had to overcome certain prejudices in their promotion of the quest for a Single Divine Language. First there was the local opinion that ancient pictograms and the tribal markers of the Ogham alphabet comprised the original form of language: while others held to the view that the first vernacular script for the continuous writing of Irish was devised and developed in the sixth century. Here the illumination of manuscripts borrowed eclectically from Italian, Spanish and North African schools and was possibly influenced by Coptic and Arabian calligraphies. Such an opinion implied that the disciples of Gallus and Columbanus were practitioners of a hybrid style, evidenced in the occurrence of convoluted ligatures, interlacing letters and large wedge-shaped serifs on the ascenders of many insular Irish scripts, including the *Gall Priscian*. It also implied that the diversity of genres, narratives, commentaries and charms found in the textual glosses of the *Priscian* was a sign of some fatal lack of cohesion. Indeed, it has even been suggested that some of these Gaelic marginalia may comprise obscure riddles and absurdities typifying the anarchic proclivities of the Hisperic grammarians – an infamous movement committed to destroying the quest for a Single Script.

1.8 The *Céle Dé* philosophy of universal brotherhood fostered by the scribes of Castledermot – and later those of St Gallen – was by no means easy. Many Irish manuscrips of the period (even the *Gall Priscian* at times) bear witness to pagan residues. Allusions to the ancient Irish Goddess, Brigid, for example, surface in the marginal comments of Máel-Patricc: a reference all the more alarming when one considers that the Origin Legend of this same Goddess constitutes Ireland's earliest pagan genealogy, attributed to a prehistoric druid; and that even after the Conversion, Brigid continued to be invoked in blasphemous terms as 'another Mary' and worshipped as 'tutelary spirit' or 'fifth province' whose legendary powers were associated with hidden wells scattered throughout Ireland and revered by druids and filí alike. Special visions were attributed to those who drank the waters from her wells. Some of the St Gallen scribes have even recorded the view that this same Brigid, so inimical to the universal Church of Rome, was the missing Sibyl of the famous Gallen collection of etchings: a thirteenth Prophetess whose pagan origins was a threat to the spirit of the Abbey and had to be expelled. The message of universal fraternity, exemplified by the quest for a single grammar for all tribes, eventually won out – though ancient scars of that battle are still traceable in the coded marginalia of the *Gall Priscian*.

1.9 The eventual triumph of the universalist philosophy of the *Céle Dé* movement was evidenced in the despatch of three outstanding Irish scholars to the three Kingdoms of Continental Europe in the ninth century, then ruled by the three grandsons of Charlemagne. Johannes Eriugena became instructor to King Charles the Bald of the Western Kingdom; Sedulius Scottus to King Ludwig of the Eastern Kingdom: and Marcellus of Ireland (Moengal) to Emperor Lothar of the Middle Kingdom. These intellectual migrations, coinciding with the transmission of the Irish *Priscian* to St Gallen, ensured the reintroduction of the unifying languages of Latin and Greek into the heart of Carolingian Europe. Three hibernian scribes, following in the footsteps of their monastic forebears, Gallus and Columbanus, became guiding counsellors to the three ruling brothers of the Continent at the very moment when the new dream of *homo universalis* was being cradled. And they were, it appears, quite conscious of this mission. Sedulius spoke of the Great Design of the Logos to unify the cosmos. Eriugena formulated a theology of the Word to found a single universe. While Marcellus professed a spiritual calling to teach at the St Gallen scriptorium as a leading authority on Scripture. All followed the vocation of Columbanus and

Gallus to re-evangelise a fragmented Europe by retrieving
the lost language of Genesis: and scholars throughout the
ages acknowledged their calling. The learned Eric of Auxerre
wrote of 'Ireland's flock of philosophers who, fearless of the
sea, came to our shores, to devote themselves to wisdom';
while the cosmopolitan rationalist, Janus Junius Toland,
celebrated 'those ancient Irish monks, famous over all the
world . . . and the schools they founded among the Picts,
Anglosaxons, Germans, Burgundians, Switzers and French;
as who has not heard of Sedulius, Columba, Columbanus,
Colmanus, Aidanus, Furseus, Kilianus, Gallus, Brendanus,
Claudius, Clemens, Scotus Erigena and numberless others'
(*The Relation of an Irish Manuscript of The Four Gospels, as
Likewise a Summary of the Ancient Irish Christianity, and the
Reality of the Keldees* in *Nazarenus*, second revised edition,
London, 1718).

2.1 The main text of the *Gall Priscian* is largely un-
problematic. It represents one of the earliest attempts
in Western civilisation to standardise the *lingua franca*
of the European empire – Latin – into a manual of
universal learning. Its sentences are linear, its paragraphs
sequential and the arguments in strict conformity with the
standard formal logic of identity and non-contradiction. It
is the marginalia that mark the *Gall Priscian* as a singular
document of its time. For it is here that the Irish scribes
interpolated their own glosses, in a mixture of Latin and
Gaelic, inscribing a coded commentary for those who would
later have eyes to read. These cryptic markings appear to
have no theological significance in their own right: there is
no logical connection between them; and often no obvious
relation between the ink letterings recorded between the
official lines of the text and the lines themselves. That is
why they were disregarded for centuries as idle jottings
of bored monks. Apart from academic interest in the first

recorded traces of Old Irish, little or no attention was paid to the actual meaning of these marginalia. The pen and ink drawings were dismissed as ornamentation and the scattered verses and charms as superfluous distractions. Any notion of hidden correspondences and interconnections was ignored.

2.2 It is for this reason that the recently discovered *Index*, representing the missing p. 241 of the original manuscript, is of such importance. Collecting as it does all the marginal fragments of the *Priscian* into a single folio (sewn together from five sheets treated with purple folium), it confirms one of my central hypotheses, namely: the single authorship of the *Gall Priscian* by Máel-Patricc whose uniform hand is in evidence throughout the *Index*. Furthermore, his decision to group the marginalia together in a sequential concordance at the end of the text indicates a single coded logic. The unified *Index* suggests a unified purpose.

2.3 It remains to be discovered, of course, what exactly this purpose might be. But it is the firm persuasion of this editor that it is none other than the transmission of the code of the perfect language – the search for which dominated early and medieval Christendom from Castledermot to Constantinople. *Phoné Semantiké Theou. Vox Domini. Gairthigern*. These were first names for the 'Voice of the Lord' – the Voice which conquered darkness and resounded throughout the cosmos during the Seven Days of Creation. The Voice which, after Adam's Fall, survived in the secret letters of the *Sefer Yetzirah*. The Voice lost forever, it seemed, after the division of language into seventy-two tongues at Babel. But if it is true that Christianity promised to bring the coveted *Logos* of God back into the world, then it must have lived on in some covert form even after Christ returned to the Father.

2.4 The key to Máel-Patricc's code is, I submit, already hinted at in the first gloss recorded in the *Index*. It refers to the following line in the main text of the *Priscian*: PHILOSOPHERS DEFINE VOICE AS VERY FINE AIR WHICH HAS BEEN STRUCK OR AS A SOUND/WHICH ESPECIALLY STRIKES THE EAR. The gloss to this sentence reads, in a mixture of Latin and Old Irish – CITABIAT CHLÚASA/CADO, ACCIDO/ VOX. Which translates roughly – EARS PERCEIVE/ TO FALL. FALL UPON/ VOICE. It is my contention that the allusion here to 'voice', 'ears' and 'perceive' refers to the lost language of *Gairthigern*, the legend of which every learned Irish monk of the period, including the scribe Máel-Patricc, would have known by heart. The scribe's etymological play on CADO/ACCIDO appears to allude to the 'fall' of language from Eden to Babel, and to the possibility of 'falling upon' another language which might undo the Fall. It is also no doubt a subtle play on the mysterious paradox which founded St Gallen in the first place, namely, the fact that it was in 'falling' into brambles and losing his sight that Gallus heard the Voice of God – and 'fell upon' the site for his monastic settlement. A settlement which was soon to create not only the most renowned scriptorium in Christendom but also the most ambitious Carolingian blueprint for a perfect Abbey with celestial choirs, archives, cloisters and towers. A settlement so assured of its privileged calling that it dared take for its motto the claim that the Voice of God resided within its precincts – *Verbum Domini Manet Internum*. The question for scholars down through the ages has been this: Where is the 'Voice' to be found? Where in the Scriptorium, with its two thousand ancient volumes, is the 'Word of the Lord' to be located, the *Logos* that might at last resolve the riddle of the Scripts?

2.5 But how decode? The opening gloss, establishing a play between *cado/accido*, is a beginning; but no more than that.

Its intention is marred by the presence of a pen-and-ink letter P, prefacing the *cado/accido* gloss, portraying a naked crosslegged monk entangled on both sides by sibyline harpies with beaked mouths whispering in his ears and sucking at his feet and tail. The next inscription listed in the *Index* sheds further light. Ostensibly no more than another stray cluster of jottings, reinscribed just after the opening gloss in the *Index*, it lends itself to a more telling reading. The passage, in translation, reads: A ROW OF TREES SURROUNDS ME/ A BLACKBIRD SINGS TO ME/ ABOVE MY LINED PARCHMENT/ BIRDS CHANT/ HIGHEST OF ALL THE CUCKOO IN HIS GREY CLOAK/ TRULY MAY GOD PROTECT ME/ FOR WELL DO I WRITE/ UNDER THE GREENWOOD TREE. The 'blackbird' and 'grey-cloaked cuckoo' that inspire the scribe are probably references to the black-robed monks of the Bangor and Armagh schools where Máel-Patricc, like Columbanus and Gallus before him, was trained. While the 'row of Greenwood trees' surrounding and protecting him are no doubt metaphors for the shelves and parchments of the Castledermot scriptorium (made from Greenwood) where the scribe is actually copying and commenting his *Priscian* text. The Abbot of Castledermot in the ninth century, Coirpre mac Feradaig, was a fervent proponent of the *Céle Dé* preference for the Way of Learning over the Way of Flesh, which accounts for the reference to 'God protecting' the scribe from the world of chaos lying beyond the Greenwood scriptorium.

2.6 The third inscription, also in Old Irish, is about sea-invasion. It reads – I DO NOT FEAR BECAUSE THE WIND IS FIERCE TONIGHT/IT RUFFLES THE BRIGHT MANE OF THE SEA/ I DO NOT FEAR THE CROSSING OF THE CALM SEA/ BY THE FIERCE WARRIORS OF LOTHLIND. While the meaning of the verse is obvious (the scribe's assurance that marauding heathen invaders will not interrupt his work on that particular night), the allusion to the 'bright' colour of the sea is highly suggestive. The recurrence of terms such as *glé*, *glas*, *glégorm* – Latin *glaucus* – to refer to the colour of the sea which threatens destruction, recurs throughout the glosses of the *Priscian* and other texts by the same scribe. But one is confronted here with a paradox – for the very same terms are also used recurrently to denote the inks used by the scribe for transcription (creation and preservation). The standard dictionary definition of *glaucus* is 'a gleaming silver-grey bluish-green hue' generally used to describe sea or water. The *Thesaurus Poeticus Linguae Latinae* provides this example – *Ionium glaucis adspergit virus ab undis* (Lr.1.721) – and points out that the term originally derived from the name of an ancient seafarer from Anthedon transformed into an ocean deity by tasting an ink-like potion (O. Met.xiii; St Silv.III, 2, 37; Aus. Mos.275; Prop.II,26, 13). *Glaucus* was also the name of a deep-sea fish (Ov.Hal.117; Plin.32, 54, 2), and curiously enough turns up in several passages of the *Casus Sancti Galli* to describe the colour of the water monsters and wild-eyed beasts banished by Gallus from Lake Constance and the surrounding forests when he first arrived in the Valley of the Steinach in 610. It is also a term frequently associated with the colour of the St Gallen sibyls' eyes. Whether these intertextual allusions are by accident or by design, it seems impossible to ascertain.

2.7 The most obvious occurrence of the *glégorm* motif is in a fourth inscription of the *Index*. It refers to the colour of the ink used by the scribe – DUB GLÉGORM. This is translated as 'a beast-coloured draught of bright-blue ink' and derives from the opening verses of the Old Saint's Song which reads as follows: MY HAND IS WEARY WITH WRITING/MY SHARP GREAT POINT IS NOT THICK/MY THIN-BEAKED PEN SPURTS FORTH/A BEAST-COLOURED DRAUGHT OF BRIGHT-BLUE INK/ . . . ON THE PAGE IT POURS ITS

DRAUGHT/OF INK FROM THE GREEN-SKINNED HOLLY. The fact that both of the opening stanzas end with old Irish synonyms for *Glaucus* – *Glégorm* (bright-blue) and *chnesglais*(green-skinned) – suggests that the scribes were aware that the blue-green ink of their manuscripts, devoted to the pursuit of perfection, was the only antidote to the blue-green eyes of pagan sea-beasts and sibyls (also referred to as *glaucus*). Near the poison you will find the cure. Sacred poison against evil poison. Script as cure for the idleness of images. Writing as *pharmakon* and *virus* – venom remedying venom. The only answer to the fallenness of flesh, brought about by Eve and her sibylline followers, is to be found in *Gairthigern* – the voice of the Lord, the Word of Scripture, the Perfect Language. The blue-green inks of sacred lettering, seeking the perfection of the skies, alone redeem the blue-green depths of the heathen-marauding seas.

2.8 This reading appears to be confirmed, as it happens, by the fifth major gloss listed in the *Index* – AD TRANSMIGRATIONEM BABYLONIS – a reference to the transmigration of Babylon which, the Bible tells us, was fourteen generations after David and fourteen generations before Christ. This strongly suggests the scribe's intention to link the transmission of redemptive ink, from manuscript to manuscript, with the transmission of the sacred seed of Abraham, from generation to generation, passing through David to Christ and the messianic promise of a Perfect Word returning to the world. The fact that I have not yet been able to locate the original occurrence of this *Index* gloss does little to discredit my reading. For the gloss does occur in the *Book of Armagh*, transcribed at roughly the same period as the *Gall Priscian*, and signed with one of Máel-Patricc's synonyms, Ferdomnach. The fact that all these glosses share exactly the same character of line-drawn initials, clear word spacing, clipped minuscule and sharp pen angle, is evidence that we are dealing with the same Armagh-tutored hand. The hand of the original master, Máel-Patricc, who wrote in Castledermot but was trained in the Armagh scriptorium as his name suggests. The logical sequential relation between the above five glosses, as listed in the *Index*, indicates the desire of the scribe to link the quest for a perfect Grammar with the search for the lost 'Voice of God', fragmented after the Fall and Babel, but transmitted through biblical generations to the birth of Christendom and the promise of the Word's Second Coming.

2.9 Finally, we might ask what, if anything, does this discovery of the glossary *Index* tell us of the life of Gallus and Columbanus? While there would seem to be no immediate connection, closer inspection yields some hints. I have already alluded to the uncanny resemblance between the *cado/accido* wordplay which opens the *Priscian* gloss and the mystery of falling/falling upon which exemplified Gallus's founding of his famous scriptorium. Can it be an accident, I ask, that the Life of Gallus originally penned by Walahfried Strabo in 833, and added to by scribes such as Konrad of Pfaefers, Kuchimaister and Ekkehart IV, is called the *Casus Sancti Galli*? And can it be an accident that this term *Casus* comprises such diverse meanings as fall, chance, plight, misfortune, event, occasion, condition, cause? The 'cause' of Gallus, as promoted by his scribal disciples, is also the 'fall' of Gallus. His rise is his descent. His failure his triumph. The *Casus* contains various accounts of the events in Gallus's life, from his birth and education in Ireland to his travels with Columbanus through the Continent, his founding of the hermitage in St Gallen, and finally his death at the age of 95 when his death-cell was invaded by a shoal of fish and his body borne off by a bevy of untamed horses. While these legends were locally interpreted as nature's final revenge on the holy monk – for expelling wild beasts from the locality of Bregenz and stealing Fridiburga from her pagan Prince – the scribes who wrote the *Casus* point out that they were nothing but superstitious rumours. The *Casus* proves that there is a correspondence between the perfect life and the perfect grammar. It relates how the search for the 'secret alphabet' of Yahweh, lost after the Fall, was brought back to Europe by Gallus and his disciples, promoting the dream of a Universal Tongue which would undo the harm of Babel and unite all warring tribes. It is this on-going mission of the Word, passed down from Abraham to Gallus, from the hidden *Book of Creation* to the quest for the Script of Scripts, which the glosses of the *Gall Priscian* seek to signal. That is the secret message the newly-discovered *Index* strives to communicate. The whole point of Gallus's life was that he had to fall, renouncing flesh, abandoning the earth, in order to devote his mind to the quest for the Perfect Language. His fall was no misfortune. The *Casus* was no accident. It was the voice of Providence summoning the foundation of the greatest scriptorium of medieval Christendom – a sacred cloistered space – to house the *Gall Priscian* with its glossed code for the Script of Scripts. I believe the key to this code is at last at hand with the rediscovery of the missing *Index*, lost for over a thousand years. If this code can be finally deciphered then one of the oldest secrets of Western spirituality may be uncovered – the hidden alphabet of Genesis, the unheard 'Voice of Yahweh'; what the ancient Irish scribes called *Gairthigern*. The *Index* has laid the sequence of glosses before us. It is now a question of reading between the lines. The meaning awaits us.

> TRULY MAY GOD PROTECT ME
> FOR WELL DO I WRITE
> UNDER THE GREENWOOD TREE

(Br. Tobias Toland, Columbanus Abbey, August, 1977)

∫

APPENDIX II

NIGHT FRAGMENTS

A: SCRIPTURES

He is set for the fall and the rising of many . . . and a sword shall pierce your heart. (Luke 2)

He who loses his life for my sake will find it. (Matthew 16)

When it says 'He ascended', what did it mean but that he had also descended into the lower parts of the earth. (Ephesians 4)

The word of God is sharper than a two edged sword . . . all are naked and laid bare to his eyes. (Hebrews 4)

I will spread my net over him . . . and I will unsheathe the sword. (Ezekiel 12)

While we live we are always being given up to death for Jesus's sake. (Corinthians 4)

Christ emptied himself . . . humbled himself and became obedient unto death. (Philippians 2)

Unless a wheat grain falls on the ground and dies . . . (John 12)

I kill and I make alive . . . when I whet my flashing sword and my hand takes hold of judgment. (Deuteronomy 32)

I went down to the potter's house and there he was working at his wheel. The vessel he was making of clay was broken in the potter's hand, and he reworked it into another vessel . . . 'Can I not do with you, O house of Israel, just as the potter has done?' (Jeremiah 18)

Because you compare your mind with the mind of God, therefore, I will bring strangers against you . . . thrusting you down to the Pit, and you shall die a violent death in the heart of the seas. (Ezekiel 28)

If it had not been the Lord who was on my side . . . the flood would have swept me away, the torrent would have gone over me; then over me would have gone the raging waves. (Psalm 124)

Should you pass through the sea, I will be with you; or through rivers, they will not swallow you up. (Isaiah 43)

Deep is calling on deep/in a roar of waters:
Your torrents and all your waves/swept over me.
My soul is thirsting for God/the God of my life;
My tears have become my bread/by night, by day,
As I hear it said . . .
'Where is your God?'. (Psalm 44)

B: SAGES

One Abyss calls the other . . . Nothing lives without dying. God himself, if He wants to live for you must die. How do you think, without death, to inherit life? (Angelus Silesius)

Throw everything away. Seek not God outside yourself but in your own soul. Withdraw into the great chamber of the soul. Sit quiet. (Meister Eckhart)

Death is the great opportunity no longer to be I . . . To die willingly, to die gladly, is the prerogative of the resigned, of him who surrenders and denies the will to live . . . he needs and desires no continuance of his person. The existence we know he willingly gives up: what he gets instead is in our eyes NOTHING because our existence is with reference to that, NOTHING . . . If (nature's) children fall, they fall back into her womb where they are safe, therefore their fall is a mere jest. (Schopenhauer)

Spirit is not the life that slinks from death . . . It wins its truth only when, in utter dismemberment, it finds itself . . . Spirit is power only by looking the negative in the face and tarrying with it. This tarrying with the negative is the magical power that converts it into being. (Hegel)

He whose eye chances to look down into the yawning abyss becomes dizzy . . . Dread is the dizziness of freedom when it gazes down into its own possibility. (Virgilius Haufniensis)

Silence is the snare of the demon; but silence is also the mutual understanding between the Deity and the individual. (Johannes de Silentio)

C: POETS

That I may rise, and stand, o'erthrow mee, and bend
Your force, to breake, blowe, burn and make me new . . .
Take mee to you, imprison mee, for I
Except you 'enthrall mee, never shall be free.
Nor ever chaste, except you ravish mee. (John Donne)

*Why should we honour those who die on the field of battle? A man
may show as reckless a courage in entering the abyss of himself.*
(W. B. Yeats)

*Sing, Heavenly Muse . . .
Instruct me, for thou know'st, thou from the first
Wast present, and with mighty wings outspread
Dove-like sat'st brooding over the vast abyss
And mad'st it pregnant: what in me is dark
Illumine, what is low raise and support.*
(John Milton)

D: From the RULE OF ST COLUMBANUS

VIII: OF DISCRETION

(IX) How necessary discretion is for monks is shown by the
mistake of many, and indicated by the downfall of some who
have been unable to complete a praiseworthy life; since, just
as error overtakes those who proceed without a path, so for
those who live without discretion intemperance is at hand
. . . (X) Therefore we must pray God continually that He
would bestow the light of true discretion to illumine this
way, surrounded on every side by the world's thickest
darkness, so that His true worshippers may be able to
cross this darkness without error to Himself. So discretion
has got its name from discerning between good and evil,
after evil began through the devil's agency to exist by the
corruption of good, but through God's agency Who first
illumines and then divides. Thus righteous Abel chose
the good, but unrighteous Cain fell upon evil . . . (XI)
True discretion cleaves to Christian lowliness and opens
the way of perfection to Christ's true soldiers, namely by
ever discerning correctly in doubtful cases.

IX: OF MORTIFICATION

(XIV) The chief part of the monk's rule is mortification, since indeed we are enjoined in Scripture, Do nothing without counsel, Ask thy father and he will show thee. A man should always hang upon the lips of another – for a person without a confessor is like a body without a head . . . If, in following this pursuit, the monk has wished to nourish any of his own desires, at once occupied and wholly confused by concern for these intrusions, he will not always be able to follow thankfully where the commandment leads . . . The part of the monk is ever to say to a senior, however adverse his instructions, Not as I will but as thou wilt, following the example of the Saviour Who says, I came not to do My will but the will of Him Who sent Me, the Father.

X: OF THE MONK'S PERFECTION

Let the monk live in a community under the discipline of one father. Let him complete the tale of his work. Let him believe that whatever his superior commands is healthful for himself, and let him not pass judgement on the opinion of an elder to whose duty it belongs to obey and fulfil what he is bidden, as Moses says, Hear, O Israel, and the rest.

ʃ

APPENDIX III

ADDENDUM TO THE *PRISCIAN* AND *INDEX*

The palimpsest of the *Priscian* consists of fourteen lines, beginning with the stray couplet of the original *Index* and moving from the centre of the parchment to the base –

AD TRANSMIGRATIONEM BABYLONIS
DUB GLÉGORM
GAIRTHIGERN SCRIPSIT
Š POST BABYLONEM NOX VENIT
7 MUNDUS IN OBSCURITATEM CECIDIT
USQUEQUO VERBUM CARO FACTUM EST
7 LUX DEI REDDITA EST

GALLUS SANCTUS HIBERNIAE
GAIRTHIGERN QUAESIVIT
Š IN OBSCURITATEM CECIDIT
♀ VERBUM CARO FACTUM NON AGNOSCENS
– VERBUM INCARNATUM –
IN MARE GLAUCO ESSE
≠ SANCTI GALLI CASUS

Fourteen lines in two verses. Fourteen for the fourteen generations separating the great cycles of the Bible, from

Abraham through Babylon to Christ, as the first line informs us. To decipher the remainder of the palimpsest we must convert the Tironian codes into roman – Š for sed, ♀ for quia, ≠ for enim, 7 for et. The verse then reads:

UP TO THE TRANSMIGRATION OF BABYLON
BLUE-GREEN INK
INSCRIBED THE VOICE OF THE LORD
BUT AFTER BABEL NIGHT CAME
AND THE WORLD FELL BLIND
UNTIL WORD BECAME FLESH AGAIN
AND GOD'S LIGHT RETURNED

GALLUS WAS A SAINT FROM IRELAND
WHO HUNGERED FOR THE VOICE OF GOD
BUT HE FELL BLIND
BECAUSE HE COULD NOT SEE
THE WORD-MADE-FLESH
IN THE BLUE-GREEN SEA
– THAT WAS THE FALL OF GALLUS.

(*Note added by Abbot Anselm, Columbanus Abbey, Sept. 1977*)

Good Benito
ALAN LIGHTMAN

'GOOD BENITO deserves a read as soon as you can get hold of it . . . an outstanding novel that captures the scientific mind-set to perfection. Spare as a set of differential equations, lucid as a watercolour, his stripped-down prose follows the uncertain trajectory of a young physicist whose intense inner life must remain incomprehensible to those unable to grapple with the maths . . . Lightman's extraordinary achievement is to weave his acute observations of the frail and the fat of a heat-soaked southern city into a book about minds, about science in its broadest sense and the way we must solve problems before we can make sense of the world'
New Scientist

'His first work of fiction, EINSTEIN'S DREAMS, was a magic realist *tour de force*; his second, GOOD BENITO is a moving and brilliant coming of age novel . . . the novel's virtues are numerous'
Sunday Telegraph

'This elegantly written novel . . . nicely balances its predecessor'
Literary Review

SCEPTRE

Dixie Chicken
FRANK RONAN

'The nearest thing Ireland has to a Martin Amis ..
From the first startling death with the blasting stereo
and the damaged brakes one is led compulsively, and
often hilariously, through a landscape that includes
incest, adolescent despair, drug abuse, suicide fixation,
sex killers, corrupt politicians, repulsive old lechers,
necrophiliacs, unfrocked priests'
Briege Duffaud in the Independent

'An enthralling mystery as well as an effective satire.
Its blasphemy makes *The Satanic Verses* look like, well,
chicken-feed; but it is also thought-provoking and
hugely entertaining'
Anthony Gardner in the Daily Telegraph

'A wonderful book, highly recommended . . . A deeply
funny tale of sex, death, corruption and infidelity,
narrated by none other than God . . . Ronan is a very
gifted storyteller'
Time Out

SCEPTRE

The Chess Garden

or

The Twilight Letters of Gustav Uyterhoeven

BROOKS HANSEN

In Ohio in 1900, Dr Uyterhoeven's wife receives a series of strange letters from her elderly husband: he reports that after being shipwrecked on the way to South Africa, he has found the legendary Antipodes, a fantastical country inhabited by warring chess pieces, dominoes and dice. Gradually the story of his life unfolds and the letters' significance becomes clear, in a tale of spiritual progress wrought with dazzling imagination.

'Wonderfully bewitching . . . reminiscent, in its colourful muscularity, of such fabulists as Borges or Calvino'
Times Literary Supplement

'The highly absorbing and endlessly inventive fiction of Uyterhoeven's adventures in the antipodes is, in fact, an allegorical examination of his spiritual principles . . . Hansen has created not one, but two imaginative delights'
The Times

'Rare and exciting . . . a complex and powerful work that achieves meaning in the most indelible way possible, through being an extraordinarily well-told tale'
Publishers Weekly

SCEPTRE